Rocking Horse Cowboys
By Pamela Stone

Rocking Horse Cowboys

Text copyright @ 2013 Pamela Stone

All Rights Reserved

DEDICATION

This is a little out of the ordinary as I'm dedicating this book to a man I've never met. Years ago, before I sold my first book, before I even had the courage to submit my first book, I saw an interview with Billy Ray Cyrus. He was talking about believing in your dreams and setting goals. Not being afraid to fail, because every time you failed, you eliminated one way that wouldn't work and were one step closer to the one way that would. Listening to Billy Ray's story gave this incredibly shy introvert the courage to believe in my dreams and to put my writing out there for others to read. Thank you, Mr. Cyrus.

Rocking Horse Cowboys

TABLE OF CONTENTS

Prologue

Chapter One

Chapter Two

Chapter Three

Chapter Four

Chapter Five

Chapter Six

Chapter Seven

Chapter Eight

Chapter Nine

Chapter Ten

Chapter Eleven

Chapter Twelve

Chapter Thirteen

Chapter Fourteen

Chapter Fifteen

Chapter Sixteen

Partners By Design (Coming June 2013)

ABOUT THE AUTHOR

Prologue

"No damn way!" Dylan McKeon blinked at the lawyer then turned his glare on his mother. "Did you instigate this?"

Daisy grinned back at him with all the innocence he knew his mother did not possess. "I'm as surprised as you, sweetie. Who'd have thought your father would do such a thing?" Judging by the upturned corners of her glossed lips, she did.

"Why would Dad leave half the ranch to Jordan?" It made no sense. Jordan had walked out of Dylan's life over two years ago and he hadn't seen neither hide nor hair of her since. Dylan turned back to the lawyer. "Is that all? What other death bed insanity did he pull?"

His father's attorney and longtime drinking buddy ran a finger down the paper and flipped the page. "A few specified items and his vast music collection he left to Daisy." He nodded to Mom. "All other personal property, vehicles, farm equipment, livestock, bank accounts go to Dylan McKeon, his only son. With the one specification."

Dylan swallowed the bile in his throat. No way in Hell he was going to allow Jordan Harris to reap a cent off of his or his father's hard work. "Fifty percent of the McKeon family's ranch? We'll see about that."

Chapter One

Jordan unsnapped the twins from their car seats and lifted them out one at a time to stand on the drive. "Wait for Mommy." Hoisting her laptop case over one shoulder and the boys' huge diaper bag over the other, she retrieved her purse and locked the car. "Ready?"

She took Trevor's hand and bent down to nudge Tristan along. The action caused the diaper bag to slip off her right shoulder. Using it as a padded buffer, she herded Tristan away from her mother's rust colored Chrysanthemums and toward the back door. "Come on, Tristan. Let's get inside out of this chill."

Maybe because they'd been premature, but they were highly susceptible to colds. "In the house, boys."

Trevor toddled up to the door, but Tristan was intent on checking out the russet fall blooms.

The wind caught Jordan's jacket and she clamped her arm against her side to keep it in place. Slinging the diaper bag back over her shoulder, she wrestled the kitchen door open and urged Trevor inside. "Wait right there while I get your brother."

She piled her stuff on the chair and went back for Tristan. "Don't pick Grandmother's flowers. Pretty to look at, but we don't touch."

She scooped him into her arms, carried him inside and closed the door. What a day. She sat Tristan beside Trevor and glanced at the clock. Almost 6:30 and she hadn't slowed down since her alarm had gone off at 5:00 this morning. But this was Wednesday, her parents' bridge night at the club. The one night each week she looked forward to her and the kids having the house to themselves.

She took each toddler by the hand and started toward the living room. Her father was on the phone in his small study and didn't even look up as she passed, but Mom bustled across the room and picked up Trevor. "Here, let me help you with them."

Relinquishing her hold on one twin, Jordan held on to the other one's hand. "Thanks, Mom."

Together, they managed to get the boys into the nursery and out of their jackets. Jordan laid Tristan down for a dry diaper. "What do you guys want for dinner tonight? Green beans?"

Tristan rolled his head back and forth. "No!"

"Broccoli?" Jordan offered.

"Uuck!" the boys said in unison.

"How about roast and potatoes?" Mom chimed in.

Judging by Trevor's smile, they'd finally hit on something he'd eat. Always the pickier eater, Tristan wrinkled his nose. "Tease."

"Cheese." The doorbell rang, but Jordan ignored it and ruffled Tristan's dark hair. "You're going to turn orange if you don't learn to eat something besides cheese."

"Well, Halloween is sneaking up on us. Maybe we should dress him as a pumpkin." Mom finished changing Trevor's diaper and snapped him back into his romper.

"Now there's an idea." Jordan smiled as she placed Tristan on the play rug beside Trevor and cocked an ear toward the living room. Her father's clipped tone indicated an unwelcome visitor.

"I didn't come to see you," a husky voice drawled.

Jordan clasped her hand over her mouth. Her heart stopped beating, and then threatened to pound a hole in her chest.

Dylan McKeon.

She'd recognize his southern drawl anywhere.

Her ears strained to catch the next words coming from the living room.

"I need to speak to her."

"Jordan has nothing to say to you." Her father's tone remained calm, but his typically quiet volume was elevated.

"Mom, could you keep the boys in here? And quiet?"

Her mother nodded. "We'll be fine."

Jordan hurried out of the nursery, closed the door, and then paused at the living room doorway. Dylan's back was to her, but there was no mistaking those wide shoulders. They dwarfed the room and threatened to sap every last ounce of air from it. Or maybe it was just her.

"Don't mean to be disrespectful, but my business is with Jordan."

Her mouth went dry and she gripped the doorframe. Wh...why? She couldn't think of one reason why Dylan would show up after this long. He hadn't cared enough to come after her when she'd left, so why now, two years later?

"Look, Mr. McKeon," her father said. "You took an impressionable young girl and led her astray. Was that not enough for you?"

Young girl? She'd been twenty-two and a college graduate. It seemed like a lifetime since she'd defied her father and climbed on the back of Dylan's motorcycle. Scared to death leaving the only home she'd ever known, yet her heart pounding with anticipation.

"Jordan was of age and left of her own accord," Dylan said.

"You were pushing thirty." Her father's expression remained cold. "You'd been in the military, seen the world, and she was a vulnerable girl."

Even as a mother of two, she still wasn't an adult in her father's eyes.

Hands on hips, Dylan squared his shoulders.

She had to do something. Opposite personalities, yet both men were hardheaded and barely tolerated one another. Gathering her wits, Jordan prayed for strength to hold herself together long enough to resolve whatever had brought Dylan to Connecticut and get him back to Texas where he belonged.

She stepped fully into the room. "Dad, I'll handle this."

Dylan turned. She forced one foot in front of the other until she was close enough to look into those smoky gray-green eyes. The left one narrowed. Never a good sign.

"Jordan."

"Hello, Dylan." *Keep your voice calm. Don't let seeing him again get to you. You can do this.* "What unfinished business?"

He leveled a glare on her father, but of course, Dad didn't offer to give them privacy. She wasn't sure she wanted him to.

Dylan sucked in a breath and turned back to Jordan. "My father passed away a month ago. In his will, he left half the ranch to me and half to you."

Her mind spun. Mac McKeon dead? She owned half his ranch?

Dad tried to step between her and Dylan. "No man in his right mind would leave property to his son's summer fling."

Jordan gulped at the word fling. At the time, she'd thought their love was strong enough to last a lifetime. *Focus, Jordan.*

"My father's reasons are irrelevant," Dylan said. "I want the title to my ranch."

She flashed her dad a pleading look. "Dad."

He took a step back, but Jordan knew what he was thinking. The calculator in her father's brain was in hyper mode trying to determine how much money they could squeeze out of this situation.

Jordan still couldn't fathom Mac being dead. He was larger than life. As was his son. "I'm sorry about your dad."

Dylan shrugged. "Thanks."

His stare was so intense, Jordan closed her eyes, shielding her thoughts from the one man who had the uncanny ability to read them. "I know you guys had your problems, but I also know how much you loved your father, and he, you."

Dylan jabbed his left hand through his hair, drawing her attention to the new shorter style. Although still thick and a little long, it no longer touched his shoulders. This style was...less rebellious.

A door closed down the hall, snapping Jordan out of her musings. She had to get Dylan out of this house and she had to do it now. "I'll sell you my half of the ranch for a dollar. Or whatever the cheapest, most expedient way to accomplish title transfer is. Just have the papers drawn up."

Again that left eye narrowed. "Just like that?"

"Dylan, I have no idea what Mac was thinking, but we both know the ranch is rightfully yours." She flinched as something solid, like one of Tristan's molded trucks, banged into the wall. She glanced nervously toward the hall. "But I have plans tonight, so if that's all...."

She took a couple steps toward the front door, turned and waited for him to follow. Still, he stood there, staring right through her. She held her ground, didn't look away. *Just leave. Please.* "Have the papers drawn up and I'll sign whatever you need."

She checked her watch as if worried about time.

Her dad stood to the side. At least he was giving her the leeway to handle this.

Why didn't Dylan just go? Being here had to be as painfully awkward for him as it was for her. After an excruciatingly long pause, he edged toward the door.

Rocking Horse Cowboys

She failed miserably at diverting her eyes from the butt of his jeans as he passed. Couldn't he saunter that faded denim any faster?

He made it onto the stoop, but before she could politely close the door, he turned. "Jordan, I..."

"Look." She tried to sound chipper. "I understand your concern about the ranch, but you didn't have to come all the way from Texas. Just mail me the papers." She glanced again at her wrist. "I really have to run."

He touched the tip of his tongue to his top lip, then closed his mouth. Obviously he had more to say, but he turned and headed toward the car parked at the curb.

Jordan shut the door and leaned her hands against it, bracing her forehead and closing her eyes. Just let him get on a plane and return home. Tonight.

Dylan had just been standing in her living room. Here, in her house. Face to face.

"You are not signing anything." Her father's voice jarred her. "Not until we research our options. You have your children's futures to consider."

Her world had every chance of imploding, and her father was focusing on money? Siphoning her last drop of composure, she turned. "Dad, this isn't open for discussion."

"Don't take that tone with me. Your irresponsibility created this mess. If it's beyond you to make logical decisions in order to protect yourself and your children, then I'll do it for you. That Texas sinkhole must be good for at least a few thousand."

If he had any idea that the ranch was almost two-hundred acres with two houses, stables, sheds...From what Jordan had seen during the few months she'd lived there, the property, even run down, was worth close to a million.

"Dad, as you've pointed out on numerous occasions, the last thing I or the boys need is Dylan back in my life."

"True. But before, the man had no money. Invested wisely, your half of that ranch would start a nice college fund for the twins."

"Unless something has changed, and I can't imagine that it has, Dylan is as cash poor as his father was. Mac bought the ranch decades ago when he was a young, championship rodeo cowboy, but if it ever turned a profit, I didn't see it. And even if it did, it doesn't matter. It belongs to Dylan."

"This subject is not closed." He squeezed the bridge of his nose. "You should feed the boys. Your mother and I are late to the club."

Dismissed. Fine. She gathered her belongings from the kitchen and hauled them down the hall. Quickly, she deposited her purse and laptop in her bedroom and then carried the diaper bag into the nursery. She pasted on a smile and patted her mother's shoulder. "Thanks, Mom. I've got them. Dad's waiting on you."

"Are you okay?" Margaret Harris took the bunny Trevor offered then turned to Jordan. "What are you going to do?"

The lump in Jordan's throat was bigger than Connecticut, maybe even Texas. She massaged her temples. "Sign the ranch over. Hope for the best. Mac must have been drunk to do such a thing."

Mom handed her the bunny. "Everything will work out."

Jordan watched the door close behind her, but Trevor's scream and Tristan's shrill, "Mine!" startling her back to reality.

"Tristan, go to time out."

Tristan dropped his little lip down, narrowing one eye and looking very much like his father. He grudgingly climbed onto the upholstered rocker, still clutching a red plastic train as his brother continued to wail.

She took the train and placed it on top of the dresser then Tristan began to wail louder than Trevor. "You know better than to snatch toys."

Dropping down on the floor, Jordan snuggled a hiccupping Trevor against her, thankful for the first opportunity of the day to actually breathe. Yes, the twins were tired and hungry and irritable, but she could relax with them. They didn't care how she was dressed or whether she made an A in her advanced psychology class. The only expectation they had of her was love.

"It's okay baby. Don't cry." But tears trickled down her own cheeks. As exhausted as she was, she could only think of one thing, protecting their secure little world.

She had to handle this situation carefully. Dylan McKeon was the one man who had the capacity to completely derail her and the boys' lives. At her slightest misstep, he could, and would turn her perfect plans into a horrific train wreck.

* * *

Jordan sat in the rocker, one sweet smelling, pajama clad twin on each leg and a book held so the kids could see. She attempted to sound like a down and out bear. At least the few words on the page were in large print. Her eyes burned from crying earlier, probably irritated further by the flecks of mascara that even with all the tears, she couldn't seem to cry out.

Tristan pointed to the donkey. "Key!"

They loved any book about animals, even cartoon sketched ones. Stretching to the floor, she picked up the fuzzy donkey puppet Trevor had dropped and bounced it across each of the boys' laps.

Trevor giggled and began to jabber and point to the donkey in the book, allowing Jordan's mind to wander. Maybe her father was right. Maybe she should think about the boys. Whatever that property was worth, her portion could certainly serve as a nice nest egg for them. No way. Her conscience would rebel. That ranch had been in the McKeon family since before Dylan was born.

Turning the page, Jordan took a deep breath. With any luck the boys would sleep through the night. They were still full from dinner, clean, and had to be tired from daycare activities. She had a couple hours case work to complete, but she wasn't sure she could focus tonight even if the boys did go to sleep early.

The doorbell chimed. Two times in one night. She wasn't expecting anyone. She placed the boys on the floor with the book. All the other doors down the hall were shut and she'd see them if they came out of the room. "You guys stay here and finish your book. Mommy will be right back."

She flipped on the porch light and put her eye to the tiny peep hole, prepared to tell whoever it was that she wasn't buying whatever they were selling. "Dylan!"

Quickly she slipped the donkey puppet behind her and opened the door part way, struggling to kick start her stalled heart. He was supposed to be gone, back to Texas or at least back to his hotel.

Without waiting for an invitation, he stepped into the room.

Jordan curled her hand into a fist and prayed the toy didn't jump out of her trembling hand. *Concentrate, Jordan.*

"I think it's time you leveled with me." Dylan took a step closer, intent on his goal.

A sharp ache stabbed Jordan in the gut. "About what? I agreed to sign the ranch over."

Dylan's gaze scorched through her. "Why are you so jumpy?"

"I'm not." She turned so he wouldn't see the toy puppet and stared at his chest, anything to avoid those eyes.

"Am I interrupting something?" Dylan continued.

"Yes. I was just about to..."

Dylan shook his head. "Yeah, not buying it."

"Well, I..." She did not have to make excuses for her actions. "What do you want?"

He shrugged, and that eye twitched. Funny, even after this long she still recognized when he was agitated. "Settle down. I didn't come back to start anything. I just think we need to end things properly like we should have before you took off."

"Two years after we split? What could any of it matter now?" Jordan paced to the far corner of the room and turned. "We've both moved on."

"Humor me. Why'd you leave?" Dylan hooked his thumbs in his front pockets.

This was a ticking time bomb, just waiting to explode.

Realizing he was focused on her face, she stashed the donkey behind a large vase of silk cabbage roses, searching for the right words to get Dylan out of here before one of the twins popped out of the hall. Amazing that they hadn't made any noise.

Her stomach churned. "Why don't we meet tomorrow for a cup of coffee? Talk in private."

He glanced around the empty living room. "Seems pretty private now. Why have you been crying?"

She swiped at the mascara smudges beneath her eyes. From the corner of her eyes she spied Tristan lurking in the doorway. Her stomach threatened to heave. "Excuse me a minute." She stepped between Dylan and the hall, but it was too late to shield Tristan from his unsuspecting father.

Tristan peeped around her legs, curious about their visitor.

Dylan stared at the child, his jaw dropped and that telltale left eye squinted. She could hear Trevor babbling in the next room. Too late! Too late to safeguard them.

Eyes wide, Tristan screwed up his face and stretched his arms up to her. He was more outgoing than his brother, but they were both insecure around people they didn't know. Jordan stooped and lifted him into the safety of her arms.

"It's okay." Jordan hugged Tristan against her shoulder.

Dylan blinked. "He's yours?"

Jordan didn't dare look at Dylan. She couldn't. Her eyes burned and her heart shattered into pieces.

Trevor appeared in the doorway, trotted over and clutched her pant leg. He leaned against her knee and wrapped a tiny arm around her leg, surveying Dylan curiously. She placed her hand on top of Trevor's blond head and cradled him against her.

She glanced at Dylan. He looked as ashen as if he'd just witnessed some ghastly accident.

She couldn't speak as she met his eyes. Couldn't tear her gaze away. Confusion, hurt, and a world of other emotions scrolled across his face like one of those rolling stock quote marquees at her father's investment office.

Dylan turned his attention from the twins, refocusing that unwavering stare on her, shock turning to reality. "They're mine?"

Chapter Two

Dylan sucked in a deep breath before his lungs collapsed. His skin felt clammy and his ears roared like a jet engine, or maybe that was the blood rushing through his veins.

The walls closed in like a vise as he slowly approached Jordan, his eyes riveted on the child in her arms. His own eyes stared back.

The lighter haired boy clutched Jordan's leg and sucked his thumb. Dylan's chest was so tight it took a conscious effort to fill his lungs.

Jordan stood frozen, motionless like a frightened rabbit, her eyes huge. Dylan's mind spun. Months, days, years. Of its own accord, his left hand reached out and touched the dark hair of the boy staring at him like he was the boogey man. A feather soft curl circled the tip of Dylan's finger.

Jordan leaned around and captured his gaze. "Dylan, I—should have told you."

He tried to digest her words, but the room had filled with an eerie fog. He heard her, but couldn't focus on anything but the child's tiny face.

As the boy backed away from his hand, Dylan lowered it. His gaze went from the child, to Jordan, to the other boy still clinging to Jordan's leg. He blinked, and then made the trip again, his brain struggling to comprehend the message his eyes were sending.

Jordan appeared as sick and confused as he felt. He knelt down to the other little boy, but the toddler clung to Jordan tighter and buried his face in her slacks.

Dylan couldn't even smile at him. "They're mine," he repeated, trying desperately to get a grasp on reality. He stood, watching Jordan's expression for confirmation.

She nodded. "Let me explain."

"Explain?" he asked incredulously. "I have twin sons that must be close to what, a year and a half old and you want to explain? Now?"

The babies both began to fret. After all, they had no idea who he was.

"Please, not in front of the boys. Lower your voice." Jordan knelt down and cradled the second child who was now wailing. "Just give me a minute to calm them down."

Dylan remained where he was until Jordan herded the kids down the hall. He shoved his hair back and tried to get control before he put his fist through her parents' dusty green wall. His throat constricted but his mind continued to tumble. Searching for any plausible excuse for Jordan's duplicity.

Twins! He had two sons.

He could hear the babies from somewhere down the hall, but he'd just upset them more if he went to them. He couldn't properly deal with them until he had a chance to process this.

He fought a total shut down but managed to sit. He rested his throbbing forehead in his hands, then sat back and gripped the chair arms. A million thoughts tumbled chaotically through his brain.

He heard Jordan softly singing as the babies quieted. What kind of woman wouldn't tell her boyfriend he was going to be a father? He pried his fingers from the fabric chair arm, but without something to grip, his hands shook. Two innocent little boys that he didn't even know. Boys who'd looked at him as if he was a stranger. Hell, he was a stranger.

Jordan had been his life. He'd opened his soul and shared things with her that he'd never trusted another living soul with.

How the hell could she justify depriving him of something like this? He would have liked to have been there for her. Felt the babies growing inside her. Held his newborn child. He blinked. Newborn children.

Anger took hold as he realized that if not for his dad leaving half the ranch to her, he'd have had no reason to come here and she'd have never told him. He'd have never known.

He blazed through all the phases from initial trance to disbelief that he was a father, to the reality, then finally fury. The last phase settled in for the duration. No way would he ever trust Jordan again.

Slowly he stood and quietly walked down the hall. He peered into the nursery where Jordan stood between two identical white cribs in a lavish blue nursery. A lamp illuminated stars spinning across the ceiling.

His body felt as charged as a grenade, just waiting for her to say something and pull the pin. But that was overridden by the gentleness of the scene. His sons.

Jordan looked at him and put a finger to her lips, but the boys were already out. Wordlessly she motioned for him to enter.

He eased up beside her as she turned to the crib on the right and whispered. "This is Tristan. He was the first born."

Dylan held his breath and stepped close. The boy looked so tiny with his knees drawn up beneath him and his pajama clad bottom in the air. Cautiously Dylan ran one finger down the baby's cherubic face. His hand looked huge and rough against the flawless complexion.

Jordan nodded at the other crib where the fair haired twin slept, sprawled flat on his back and smacking loudly on his thumb. "And this is Trevor, arriving only three minutes after his brother and weighing in at four pounds and seven ounces. That's two ounces more than Tristan."

Bizarre to have someone tell you the names of your own kids. "Tristan and Trevor," Dylan repeated.

"They turned one last March."

As Dylan touched Trevor's feathery blond curls, his hand trembled. "He still looks bigger." He calculated the time. "So they're nineteen months?"

She nodded. "They're both slightly below scale, but they're catching up. Trevor is chunkier than Tristan. He isn't as active and he eats more, but they're healthy and on track." Jordan backed away, allowing him some space. Or just not wanting to be close to him.

Without waking up, Trevor wrapped his fist around Dylan's index finger. Dylan would have stood motionless all night to savor that touch, but after a couple minutes the tiny fingers relaxed and relinquished their hold.

He snapped a picture of each boy with his cell phone as Jordan took a stance by the door on point like a mama bird when a cat crept too close to her nest. *Jordan* didn't trust *him*?

Dylan turned as the bed creaked behind him. The darker haired child, Tristan, he reminded himself, sat up and rubbed his eyes. He stared at Dylan then screwed up his face to cry, but Jordan quickly scooped him into her arms. Tristan buried his face against Jordan's shoulder.

Ignoring the drool on her blouse, she swiveled so Dylan could get a better look at him. "Tristan, this is Dylan."

Okay, so maybe it was asking too much for her to introduce him as Papa at this stage.

Tentatively, Dylan reached out his hand, but Tristan clung to Jordan. He focused those unwavering gray-green eyes on Dylan. My god, it was uncanny how much the boy resembled him.

Dylan waited a minute and then offered him his hand again. Tristan took it, but didn't make a move to go into his arms. It would take time.

Trevor caught Dylan's attention as he clung to his crib rail, bouncing and jabbering in the general direction of Jordan.

Tristan arched his back and fretted to get down. Jordan placed him on the play rug then picked up Trevor and set him beside his brother before touching a switch on the bedside lamp. Soft light replaced the revolving stars.

Trevor made a wide circle around Dylan and picked up a stuffed rabbit from behind the door. Tristan also took a fancy to the toy and they began tugging on both floppy ears of the bunny, squealing in gibberish at one another.

Dylan flinched at the unexpected pitch. How could that much noise come out of two tiny people? Jordan didn't even seem to notice.

"They're irritable when they're tired," she said, locating an identical rabbit and holding it out. "Here, Tristan. Here's yours."

Once there were two rabbits and nothing to squabble over, they lost interest and started tossing an assortment of toys out of a blue plastic tub.

Dylan stepped closer and squatted down on their level. They needed time to get used to him, sort of like the high-spirited filly he'd been training.

But, he marveled, these weren't horses. They were his children. Geez, give him the patience to not just pull them into his arms. It was torture to be so close and yet hold back.

They took turns presenting him with toys to examine, but neither one got close enough for him to hug. He could do this. The new relationship was fragile. They'd warm up to him in time.

Dylan remained still as they did what babies do. The fact that they were offering him their treasures was a positive start. Still, it didn't take long for them to start rubbing their eyes and fussing. Probably weren't accustomed to being woken up by some strange man after they were down for the night.

He stood aside as Jordan lifted them back into their cribs and covered them with blue blankets. She kissed each on the cheek then touched the switch on the bureau lamp. Once again lighted stars swirled across the ceiling and walls.

By magic, the boys quieted and settled in. Dylan watched until they drifted back to sleep. He kissed the tip of his finger and touched it to Trevor's tiny pink mouth. "Love you," he whispered before repeating the same ritual with Tristan. And he did love them. He would've never thought it possible to fall so in love with two tiny beings instantly, but along with all the conflicting emotions right now, his heart threatened to explode.

Jordan didn't react, just tiptoed out of the room.

Dylan wasn't ready to leave, but followed. "They're...I don't even know what to say."

"You haven't been around when they're wide awake and hyped." She quietly closed the nursery door. "They can be a handful."

Dylan moved between her and the living room before she could escape. "I haven't been around them at all, because you didn't tell me they existed!"

The emotion of the evening had drained every ounce of energy from his body, but now it roared back supercharged. Jordan looked as limp as a rag doll. The only things showing any life at all were her bouncy dark curls. Shorter and a little curlier than before.

"I admit I should have told you, but could we calm down before discussing this? I'm destroyed."

"Lady, you don't know the meaning of destroyed. Step into my boots."

She flattened her back against the closed door and stared at the ceiling. "You're determined to get into this tonight?"

"Damn straight."

Jordan led the way back to the living room. "We always knew we were from different worlds," she said in that frustratingly calm, emotionless voice that used to make Dylan want to kiss her into the passionate woman he knew smoldered beneath that icy surface.

Not his mood at the moment.

"So you just didn't tell me?" His chest was going to cave in.

"Dylan, calm down. Stop yelling before you wake the boys."

He clutched the back of a chair. "Two damn years you kept this from me. And you have the audacity to tell me to calm down?"

"I understand your anger. However, this conversation would be more productive if we wait and talk tomorrow when our initial emotions have had a chance to subside."

"Don't feed me that psycho-babble. I want you to explain why you failed to mention to me that I was going to be a father."

"What was the point? It was already over between us."

He put his hands on his hips and tried to keep his voice calm. "So you knew you were pregnant when you walked out on me?"

"No, I didn't know."

"You were on the pill." He paused and shoved his hair out of his face. "Did you just decide you wanted a child, but not a husband?"

* * *

Jordan's temper bristled. She slowly counted to ten, reminding herself that losing her temper meant losing control and Dylan was a master at undermining her control. She kept her voice even. "I would never trick you. You know me better than that."

"I'm not sure I know you at all. I never would've believed you'd give birth to our babies and not even have the decency to tell me. How the hell do you justify that?" Dylan's eyes widened. "I trusted you."

"And I trusted you. But when we moved to the ranch, you changed. That wonderful, passionate man who'd swept me into an amazing fantasy was never around. You were out working the ranch and when you were home, you were arguing with your dad, or me. You were no longer the man I fell in love with." She shivered and rubbed her hands up and down her arms. But Dylan had never loved her as much as she'd loved him and certainly not enough to marry her. He'd made that clear when he hadn't so much as tried to call her after she left. And that gave him the power in the relationship. Dylan would have been able to control her, just like her father had always held over her mother until he'd sapped the last bit of vibrancy out of her.

Dylan's gaze bore into her. "No excuse. You knew what I was up against with my old man."

"Things were falling apart between us. I wasn't happy and neither were you. Right or wrong, I left."

Dylan's boots clunked across the tile floor as he paced. "Don't give me that crap! Come on, Jordan, if I hadn't shown up here, I'd never have known. You wouldn't have told me now except you had no choice."

Dylan stopped close, towering over her, his face inches away. The heat from his body made her tremble. "What did you tell your parents? That I kicked you out? Didn't want kids? They didn't have a bad enough opinion of me before?"

She tried not to be drawn into the emotion as his voice escalated. One, two, three. Deep breath.

He gritted his teeth. "Jordan, don't shut me out."

"Then stop yelling." *Stand your ground, don't retreat.* When Dylan got all wound up, he discussed...loudly.

He looked like he might explode then stared up at the chandelier and drew in a deep breath. "I'll calm down."

Jordan attempted to regain her composure. "It's really as simple as I told you. You told me that if I didn't want to be there, to go. I left. I didn't see any future for us. When I found out I was pregnant, it just seemed easiest not to tell you. The relationship was over and there was nothing to gain by reopening old wounds," she explained, modifying the facts slightly to make them more palatable. "In retrospect, I should have handled things differently, but at the time, I thought I was doing the right thing."

"The right thing! I've missed out on not only their birth, but the entire first year and a half of their lives. They looked at me like I was a stranger. Do you know how that felt? What if the situation were reversed? I know you've been brought up to hold your emotions in check, but I never realized you were heartless."

The word hit below the belt. "I'm not heartless."

They stared one another down until Jordan began to wonder whether he was even going to speak.

"I want to take them to the ranch."

"What?"

He raised his eyebrows. "Get to know them. Give them time to get used to me."

"No!" Just the idea that the twins be anywhere other than with her was unimaginable.

Dylan stuffed his hands into his front pockets and leaned toward her. "No?"

Jordan didn't back down. "No way. They're just babies. I'm their mom. I'm all they know. You can't take them away from me."

"You've had them to yourself for nineteen months. And that's not even counting the time you were pregnant. A father has rights."

"You can come here and spend all the time you want with them."

"The ranch doesn't run itself. I can't afford to stay here more than a few days."

Speaking of the ranch. Jordan took a deep breath. "Dylan, I realize you're strapped for cash and can't afford to pay child support. I have a suggestion."

He frowned. "Something tells me I don't want to hear this."

"I'll sign the ranch over to you like I agreed. You're free to do whatever you have planned for it. I'll continue to raise the boys. No child support. Nothing. We both just get on with our lives."

The determined clench to that square jaw and the way his mouth ticked caused her to second guess the wisdom of her suggestion. But she couldn't fathom being separated from her children for more than the few hours each day she spent in class or at work. Texas? Two thousand miles away from her!

Dylan grabbed his brown leather jacket off the chair. "I will spend time with my sons. If you're going to be unreasonable, then we'll make it legal."

"Then I'll keep my half of the ranch." The words flew out of her mouth in desperation. She wasn't even sure what she hoped to gain, except that maybe she could use it as leverage.

That left eyebrow of his cocked. "See you in court."

She flinched as the door slammed behind him.

Chapter Three

Jordan hadn't heard from Dylan for over a week and had almost convinced herself that he'd cooled off, decided to let it go. Like he and his father back at the ranch. They'd be yelling one minute and five minutes later, drinking coffee and joking. Maybe Dylan just got over his anger and decided that twin toddlers he didn't even know were too much trouble.

Friday afternoon she realized she'd gotten her hopes up too soon. Jordan and Cara were conducting their last family counseling session of the day, when the admin knocked on the door. "Ms. Harris, you're needed in the outer office."

Jordan's breath caught in her throat. Was something wrong with one of the boys? Janet didn't interrupt a session unless it was urgent.

Cara exchanged glances with Jordan and nodded toward the door.

Jordan smiled her appreciation and left the session as unobtrusively as she could. If she'd been able to hand pick a mentor and sponsor for her internship she couldn't have found anyone better than Cara Gryphon. The woman was a saint. Jordan eased the door closed and approached the stern young woman standing in the reception area.

"Jordan Rose Harris?"

A feeling of imminent doom filled Jordan's heart. "Yes."

"You've been served. Sign here please."

The woman didn't even change expressions as Jordan signed the receipt and took the brown envelope. She knew, without opening it, it was from Dylan. Whatever was inside wouldn't be good.

"Have a nice day." The courier slipped the signed clipboard into her satchel and made for the door.

Nice day? Right.

She'd been grasping for a fantasy to think Dylan would just walk away. Jordan might be a master of passive aggression, but Dylan McKeon didn't know the meaning of passive.

Clutching the envelope, she escaped into a vacant conference room. The twins were her life. They were the only reason she'd sucked up her pride and moved back into her parents' house. Why she functioned on five hours sleep and worked long hours to get her license.

Holding her breath, she slid one finger beneath the flap and wedged it open. Understanding legalese was beyond her, but it didn't take a law degree to figure out what Dylan wanted.

She jumped and turned toward the tap on the door. Cara peeped in. "You okay?"

Jordan shook her head. "Dylan's taking me to court. He didn't call or try to work this out. Just hired a lawyer."

Cara stepped up to the table and folded her long leggy frame into a royal blue conference chair.

Jordan scooted the papers in front of her mentor. After twenty years in the counseling profession, Cara had experience dealing with all kinds of domestic disputes.

"I can't believe he's doing this." Jordan was too agitated to sit so she paced to the window and stared out at the gray, dismal rain.

"From what I can tell, he just wants the right to take them to Texas twice a year for a month each visit." Cara patted Jordan's hand. "I understand how devastating this seems, but you have to realize the court may rule in his favor."

Jordan massaged her forehead. "I've never been this frightened."

"Frightened that the boys wouldn't be safe with him?"

Jordan blinked back tears. "No. Dylan would keep them safe. But they'd be confused and upset. They've never been away from me, not a single night since they were born."

"And you'd be lost without them?"

"A whole month? I couldn't bear it." Jordan sat next to her friend and shoved the papers aside. "Couldn't he just come here and get to know them, at least the first few times? Let them get a little older. Out of diapers."

Cara grinned. "Out of college..."

Jordan rubbed her eyes and returned the grin. "Yeah, that would be good."

"I can recommend a good lawyer."

A lawyer? One more thing she didn't have the money for without turning to her parents for assistance. Her father's attorney was excellent, but as a person he was a cold hearted jerk and not the type to consider emotional stakes. "I don't have much choice. Even if I have to go into debt, I have to protect my custody of the boys."

Cara scribbled a name on a pad lying on the table, ripped off the little yellow sticky note and handed it to Jordan. "He's good and he won't charge excessively, unless Dylan insists on dragging this out."

Jordan stared at the note, but the letters blurred through her tears. "I'd hoped he'd be reasonable, but then again, when Dylan wants something, he doesn't stop until he gets it." Once Jordan had been what he wanted.

"If the man was that difficult, how did you get along with him long enough to fall in love?" Cara grinned. "Or get pregnant?"

"Oh, you find this amusing?" Jordan had shared way too much with the woman, especially right after the twins' birth. "Dylan is an 'in the moment' guy. Whatever he's doing, he's completely focused on. Be that having fun, getting himself all worked up and angry...or making love." Jordan stopped and tried to erase that image from her mind. "After his dad had the accident, we moved to the ranch to help out. Dylan's focus shifted, on a mission to repair everything that had been neglected since he'd left. Up until then, his passion for life was positive and exciting and he swept me right along with him."

"So you were jealous of the attention the ranch stole from you?"

"That's ridiculous." Jordan twisted her hair. "It wasn't the ranch, it was Dylan. Nobody is all good or all bad. I know that. But he became a different person."

"He's just asking for visitation rights. He hasn't mentioned custody. What am I missing?"

"Money. I have none."

"Does he?" Cara tilted her head. "If it boils down to a deep pocket battle, who wins?"

Jordan shook her head. "Unless something has changed, he doesn't have excess cash lying around. But he's resourceful."

"And you own half the man's ranch."

Maybe everything did happen for a reason. "That I do. I'm not sure how to use it, but I'm not signing it over until this visitation issue is resolved."

Cara tilted her head. "Well, I do have one suggestion."

* * *

Dylan gave the wrench a hard turn and grabbed his ringing cell phone off the tractor's seat, jerking his hand back from the sun scorched steel. "This is Dylan."

Texas weather! Mid-October and still pushing ninety. Swiping the sweat out of his eyes, he gave his lawyer his full attention. "What kind of proposition?"

"Ms. Harris' attorney is suggesting that before you both drop an unnecessary amount of money taking this to court, that you try mediation. You said you didn't want to waste time. We could arrange the mediation as early as next week whereas a court date might take months."

Dylan ignored Cinder's nose nuzzling under his left armpit and tried to think. He was all for settling this and getting to know the twins before they were grown. But since the boys were Connecticut residents, everything would take place there which put the added financial burden of travel on him. At least he'd hired a Connecticut lawyer. "Are you present during mediation?"

"I can set it up either way. The most expedient method is for you and Ms. Harris to work out a satisfactory agreement on your own through the mediator. Attorneys playing a role adds cost. But still less expensive than court."

"What else should I know?"

Cinder whinnied and Dylan rubbed the horse's satin smooth neck then fished a sugar cube from his jeans pocket and held it out. Cinder took the cube, tossed his mane and raced off.

Dylan continued to listen to the lawyer as Sam bolted to his feet and chased the stallion as far as the coral gate. The German shepherd pup didn't have a snow cone's chance in August of catching the four year old thoroughbred and evidently today it was too hot to even pretend. Sam caught the milk bone Dylan tossed and stretched back out in the shade beneath the tractor.

"You just have to both go into mediation with open minds. At least the children's welfare is in the parents' control instead of a judge's."

That sounded good, but if the last time he and Jordan had spoken was any indication, the likelihood of them agreeing on even what brand of diapers to buy was probably overly optimistic.

Jordan seemed like a different person this go-round. Gone was that beautiful girl who'd spent heated nights in his arms, making love until they were both sated. Gone was the laughter and life.

Don't go there McKeon. He'd worked through this crap.

If she didn't love him enough to stick around through the rough times, fine. He was not his old man and he refused to pine away over a woman who chose to live her life elsewhere rather than with him. A mistake that had landed his father six feet under.

Don't let it get to you. Two years ago she'd disappeared leaving nothing behind but a damn note. He'd sworn then that he'd never chase her. Nothing had changed. Yeah, except he'd seen her again.

The horse kicked up dust as he galloped across the pasture, tail flying in the hot breeze. Exquisite specimen of Midnight's bloodline. Cinder hopefully would sire some prime colts and generate stud fee income. Lord knows, Dylan could use the money.

He inhaled the smell of the cows grazing in the pasture behind the barn. He'd never had any great love for cattle, but they were finally bringing in some money. This was his life now.

The attorney cleared his throat. "Mr. McKeon, are you still there?"

"Yeah."

"You're legally bound by agreements reached during mediation. If you're unable to work out an equitable arrangement, then the case will be settled it in court. Nothing lost."

Except airfare, a couple nights in a hotel and another chunk out of his already trampled heart. Dylan leaned against the tractor and tallied the money he'd dropped this week on repairs. He had to get this tractor running and the forty acres of hay harvested this week before a cold front blew in.

Conserving his limited funds was good, but mediators sounded like counselor types and that was Jordan's field of expertise. "Do we get any pull on choosing the mediator? I don't want the deck stacked against me by having someone who knows Jordan or her old man."

"It's my job to make sure that doesn't happen."

Dylan tossed his gimme cap on the tractor seat and finger combed his sweaty hair off his forehead. "Set it up."

* * *

"I can't under any circumstances allow my children to travel two-thousand miles away. And certainly not for an entire month."

"Our children." Dylan tamped down his temper, glared at Jordan across the table and talked over the mediator's attempts to keep peace. "You've made it clear that you don't want me to be part of their lives, but that is no longer your choice."

He wasn't sure what he'd expected from mediation, but this wasn't it. He'd hoped that he and Jordan could agree on how to share the boys rather than having some judge make that decision. Wasn't looking promising.

"Right or wrong, I'm the only parent they've known up until this point. Being separated from me would upset them and hamper your attempt to get to know them. Texas isn't an option."

He studied Jordan, trying to figure out how the hell a relationship that had started out so beautiful ended up here. A cold standoff between two strangers. "They have just as much reason to be in Texas as in Connecticut."

"They're twenty month old babies." Jordan leaned across the table but didn't raise her voice. Just that infuriating, cold, practical tone.

"You both have valid points." Barbara, the mediator, interjected. She looked from Jordan to him. "Let's think outside the box and possibly come up with a workable solution?"

Jordan's lips stretched into a thin line and she clasped her hands in her lap. "As long as it doesn't involve my children leaving Hartford."

"I can't afford to stay here more than a couple days. And as much as it's bound to rile your control freak personality, you no longer have the privilege of being the sole decision maker."

"I'm not a control freak. I made a logical decision that alcohol-fueled screaming matches were not a healthy environment for children." Her eyes flashed, but her voice remained controlled.

So now it was Dylan's fault that his father had been an alcoholic? "At least my dad and I communicated. Your father says jump and you and your mom ask how high. Not exactly a healthy example for kids either."

"Tossing accusations is not going to resolve this." Barbara placed both hands flat on the polished wood table. "Mr. McKeon, you want time to get to know your children and you can't afford the cost of a prolonged stay in Connecticut. Correct?"

Hadn't he just said that? "Correct."

"Ms. Harris. You've been the sole parental figure in the boys' lives and believe that they will be upset if separated from you? Correct?"

"Yes." Jordan sat back in her chair and crossed her arms over her chest. "It's a documented fact that too many changes at once have long term negative effects on children."

He honest to God saw red. "And growing up not knowing their father doesn't? Kids adjust! I'm not going away, Jordan. Deal with it."

Barbara ignored him and turned her attention to Jordan. "Is it possible that Mr. McKeon could save the cost of a hotel and stay in a spare room at your house?"

"No." Jordan shook her head back and forth. "I live with my parents."

Dylan kicked back in his chair. That was the first thing they'd agreed on. "Her father despises me. But the bigger issue is that I run a ranch. If I'm away, it's difficult to find someone to tend to things."

"Then who would watch the boys?" Jordan demanded. "They can't exactly tag along from sunup until sundown while you're doing whatever it is you do."

Oh, like he'd just leave them in the house to their own devices. Unbelievable. "My mom is waiting on the phone to ring to get to know her grandkids."

"Just one more unfamiliar person. You can't yank them up and transport them into your world and expect everything to be okay. They don't know you."

"Don't toss that in my face! Kind of difficult to be a part of their lives when I didn't know they existed." What had he done to make this woman hate him? Granted, the atmosphere at the ranch had gotten a little heated, but she'd just left. Just like his mother, when things got rough, she was outta there. Zero commitment! "You left me, lady!"

"Accusations aren't accomplishing anything here," Barbara said. "This is about the children and what's best for them. They have a father, whether they've grown up knowing him or not, and he wants to remedy that."

"I'm not arguing his right to get to know them. But small children are devastated by prolonged separations from their mother." Jordan stood and paced.

"They would be? Or you would?" The horse he'd rescued last month had been easier to work with than her. "This isn't about you, counselor Jordan."

"You both need to calm down." Barbara pointed Jordan toward a chair. "What if Mr. McKeon took the twins to Texas?" Jordan started to speak, but Barbara silenced her with one finger. "Ms. Harris would accompany the boys during the initial visit which would allow them to get to know their father while maintaining the security of their mother."

No way! Spend a month with Jordan in his home? There wasn't a house big enough to contain all his feelings surrounding her. He'd given Jordan his heart and at the first rough spot, she'd tossed it away as if it was horse dung. Add to that his fragile relationship with the twins. She'd interfere at every juncture. "I'm capable of taking care of my sons without her."

"Then I'm not agreeing for you to take them," Jordan said, taking her seat. "We can settle this in court."

"Works for me."

"That is certainly your choice," Barbara said. "But keep in mind that a judge will mandate the future arrangement for your children. And unlike mediation, you won't be given the option to agree or disagree."

Jordan's eyes pooled and she looked into his, clasping her hand over her mouth. Finally she blinked, as if the reality had finally penetrated. "Dylan, we have to resolve this. We can't allow some stranger to make this decision. Maybe I can arrange a couple weeks. It'll just mean that it'll take me longer to get in my intern hours."

His jaw dropped. It wasn't a month, but she was actually willing to take time out of her life to avoid being separated from the kids. Surely they could co-exist that long. "Two weeks is a start, but they'll be at the ranch to spend time with me. I won't tolerate you scrutinizing every decision I make."

"Okay." She twisted her hair, but didn't look away. "We just need to use this time to rationally determine what's best for the boys."

"Yes." Barbara let out a sigh. "Talk things through. Trust me, it's always a more loving arrangement if the parents can agree. Court is based strictly on logic and law."

So was Jordan, but he decided to let that one slide. At least he'd have time with the kids on his turf, not hers.

Chapter Four

Jordan set her purse on the massive wooden credenza just inside the front door of Dylan's log house and switched Trevor's sleeping body to her other shoulder. Her arm throbbed from his weight. So much had happened in two days since mediation.

Dylan followed her inside and pushed the door closed with his boot. He nodded to the left. "Let's put them in the small bedroom. It has twin beds and they're low to the ground." Tristan twisted in Dylan's arms and surveyed his new surroundings.

The house was just as Jordan remembered. Over-sized rooms and furniture. The exterior walls were log. The hardwood floor was scuffed from thirty years of heavy cowboy boots. And probably a few scratches from Dylan's mom's high heels when she visited. Still the worn paths added to the solid, homey feel. The house fit Dylan just as it had his father.

She couldn't imagine this house without Mac McKeon in it. She glanced at Dylan. Did he feel the emptiness?

"Ook." Tristan pointed at the stone fireplace and squirmed.

As soon as Dylan sat him on the floor, Tristan raced toward the hearth as fast as his chubby little legs would carry him, climbed up and confiscated the toy green and yellow tractor sitting on the hearth. He plopped down on the brown cushion, already turning the wheels.

Not a good toy for a toddler. "Be careful. That's metal and it has sharp edges."

"He's fine, Jordan." Dylan squatted down beside him and showed him how the steering wheel turned the front wheels. "I played with this when I was a kid."

Tristan grinned and turned the back wheels with his finger then set the tractor on the stone hearth and pushed it back and forth. "Brmbrmbrm."

Her left arm was going numb, but she wasn't about to put Trevor down to sleep in a strange room. What if he woke up and didn't know where he was? Plus his allergies had kicked in on the plane and he'd be irritable when he woke. She gently placed him on the sofa and tossed a couple of cushions down on the plank floor to cushion his fall if he rolled off. He stretched out flat on the tan leather and stuck his thumb in his mouth.

Jordan put her hands on her hips and glanced around. No way could this place be child proofed. The hearth was so low they could actually crawl into that fireplace. No telling what was sitting around at child level that could hurt them. And the way they climbed, child level was anywhere under five feet. At her parents' house the boys spent most of their time in the nursery. "I need to get the diaper bag from the car."

Tristan climbed onto the chair, buried his tiny sneakers between the ladder back rungs and pulled himself up.

Before she could get to him, Dylan wrapped an arm around his waist. "Whoa there. You're a climber."

Jordan smiled. "Wait until his brother wakes up and there are two of them to chase."

"Really." Dylan placed Tristan on the rug in front of the fireplace and handed him the tractor. "If you'll keep him off the ceiling fan, I'll unload the truck."

"Okay." She smirked as she moved a pewter tray from the coffee table to one of the shelves, hopefully out of the boys' reach. There wasn't much she could do to protect Dylan's family's antique grandfather clock, except try to keep the boys away from it. She blew out a breath, remembering lying in bed and listening to it strike six bongs every morning after Dylan left the house. How was she going to survive the next two weeks?

She confiscated the fireplace utensils and started toward the hall closet just as Dylan came in loaded with suitcases.

He frowned. "Where are you going with those?"

"They're sharp and heavy."

Without further comment, he hauled her paisley suitcase to the guest room at the front of the house. On the opposite side from where he'd suggested the kids would be.

"Why don't I sleep in your old room?" she asked as he came out. His childhood room shared a bath with the smaller bedroom...the kids' room.

He stopped, faced her, and cocked his head. "Moving a little fast, aren't we?"

Heat started at the top of her neck and spread across her cheeks. "You haven't moved into the master? I just figured since your father died."

"Nope. But feel free to sleep wherever you're comfortable."

Dylan ruffled Tristan's hair before heading out the door for more kid paraphernalia.

In spite of her best effort, images of sleeping in Dylan's huge oak bed played in her mind like some X-rated movie. Then lying snuggled in his arms until the sun turned the room to orange. How he'd smelled fresh from the shower each morning when he'd kiss her before leaving to tackle the chores.

She touched her tongue to her lip and followed him as he hauled the boys' suitcases into their bedroom. Tristan trailed after him like a puppy, eager to see what else there was to get into. Horse pictures hung on the log wall as if the room came straight out of the 50s. "Why don't the twins sleep with me in the guest room? It still has a king sized bed, doesn't it?"

"Nope, and yep. They'll be fine in here. My cousin cleaned the room and put fresh linens on the beds."

"But they aren't used to this room and they won't know where to find me. What if they cry and I don't hear them from across the house?"

Tristan crawled up on one of the beds and flashed his tiny pearly whites, defying her concern that they wouldn't feel comfortable.

"I'll hear them." Dylan placed the bag on the other bed and left the room.

"But..." There were twin beds. The boys still slept in cribs. They might tumble out of bed. Or get up and wander off, get hurt. Or not be able to sleep in strange surroundings. Or be afraid. They were used to routine. They got up at the same time, went to bed at the same time, knew what to expect.

The grandfather clock chimed the Westminster melody followed by five loud bongs.

"Mamamama."

"In here, sweetie." Jordan walked to the door. One nice thing about the house was that there was very little space wasted in hallways. Everything was centered around the large great room.

Trevor trotted into the bedroom, eyes wide. He wiped the sleep from his eyes and made a beeline toward Jordan.

She scooped him into her arms and kissed his cheek. "Hi, sleepy head." She pulled a tissue out of her pocket and wiped his nose.

Typically he'd snuggle into her shoulder, but he turned his head away from the tissue, taking in the room. He pointed to the picture over one of the beds. "Hawsssy."

She carried him closer. "What sound does the horse make?"

"Neeee," he squealed in unison with his brother, reaching out to touch the picture.

"You do realize that we paid more to check all this luggage than we did for the airline tickets, don't you?" Dylan placed the case she'd packed full of the boys' toys and the blankets they slept with in the center of the floor. He'd drawn the line at the port-a-cribs. "Is all this stuff necessary for two little bitty kids?"

She bristled. "They require a little more than a box of diapers and a change of clothes."

"Whatever you think." He unzipped the bag so the kids could dig through the toys. "You packed two of everything."

"There are two boys." She rolled her eyes. "I need to feed them soon or they'll get irritable."

Dylan shrugged. "What do they eat?"

Was the freezer still stocked with fresh vegetables from the family garden? Dylan's dad, aunt, and cousins had planted a huge truck garden the summer she'd lived here. They'd taught her to prepare the vegetables for the freezer. But even if the freezer was stocked, that food took too long to thaw. "Maybe a can of green beans or carrots? Do you have any fruit? Bananas?"

"We'll have to pick up fruit tomorrow." He held his hand out to Trevor. "You guys want to go with Papa and see what we can scrape together for dinner?"

Jordan tried not to let the word Papa throw her. At least neither twin made a move to go with Dylan and for some reason she felt that gave her a slight advantage. She took each of them by the hand. "Hungry?"

Dylan opened the bedroom door and the three of them followed him into the kitchen. The roomy open concept was the heart of the house. The kitchen was separated from the family room only by a bar with stools, making it the perfect gathering place. Huge and with all the conveniences. When Mac McKeon had built this house thirty years ago, he'd built it with family in mind. Plenty of workspace. Since she was last here, the countertops had been upgraded to dark coffee-black granite.

"I like the new counters."

"Mom talked him into them." Dylan opened the pantry and handed her a can of mixed vegetables. "Do they eat applesauce? That's the only fruit type substance I have."

Fruit type substance? "Applesauce is fine." She ran her hand over the glossy new countertop. So Mac had still been trying to please Daisy right up until the end.

There were no highchairs. She'd never get the kids to sit still in a dining chair. Tristan especially was so easily distracted, that in order for him to eat he had to be strapped in. There were too many more interesting things for him to do rather than eat. Dylan grabbed him just before he splashed water out of the dog's stainless steel water bowl. Tucking him into the crook of his arm, Dylan took a couple plates out of the cabinet and placed them on the butcher block table.

Jordan opened the vegetables and heated them a few seconds in the microwave then spooned some onto each plate. While Dylan corralled the kids, she ran to the bedroom for their toddler flatware and Sippy cups. She scooped applesauce into two small bowls, but pushed them back so the kids would eat the vegetables first.

"What do they drink?" Dylan held up the two sippy cups.

"Milk or apple juice. If you don't have that water will work." Sitting, she positioned one twin on each leg so they were tall enough to reach their plates. "Use your forks."

She grabbed Trevor's hand before he could grasp a handful of carrots. "We don't eat with our hands, mister."

Tristan picked up his fork and stabbed a green bean, but Trevor's coordination at feeding himself with a spoon was not sufficient to feed his insatiable hunger. She stabbed a couple vegetables and handed him the fork.

Dylan placed the glasses on the table and took a seat beside her. "Here, let me have one of them."

"The green cup is Trevor's." She scooted Tristan over to Dylan's lap and continued to help Trevor. He loved food and wasn't as patient at using utensils as Tristan. However, Tristan's next bite landed on Dylan's jeans.

"Geez." Dylan grabbed a napkin out of the holder in the center of the table and cleaned the green beans then took Tristan's fork and fed him a bite. "Slow down. Promise. I'm not going to steal your green beans."

Jordan was so engrossed watching Dylan's reaction, that she didn't notice Trevor shoveling his food in by the fistful until a sticky little hand smacked her wrist.

Dylan held a napkin out to him and Trevor decided if his brother was on Dylan's lap, then he should be too. Or was he trying to abscond with Tristan's food. Either way, he grabbed his father's bare arm with his grimy fist and Dylan ended up with both kids.

When the phone rang, Jordan stood. "I'll bring it to you. You have your hands full."

She clicked the phone on and held it to his ear. "Yeah, we're home." He tried to get an arm around Tristan so he could wipe Trevor's hand. "Uh, not right now. I'm up to my armpits in smushed carrots."

Before she caught herself, Jordan giggled. The frown she received in return did not mirror her amusement. "Here, let me take Tristan."

Willingly, Dylan relinquished his hold and exchanged one baby for the phone. "That'd be great. Appreciate it."

Jordan handed him a dishtowel as he hung up. He wiped the phone as she cleaned Tristan's hands and then moved the applesauce in front of each boy. She picked up the spoon and scooped a bite of colorless mush. "If you don't want that in your hair, you might just feed it to him," she suggested to Dylan.

He grinned at Trevor. "We can handle that, huh?"

Trevor bounced back and forth almost head butting Dylan in the process. He opened his mouth and took the first bite, but continued to bounce as he swallowed the applesauce without batting an eye. "Bite."

Tristan ate as she fed him, but Trevor leaned forward to meet the spoon before Dylan could get it out of the bowl with the next bite.

Trevor had just finished when there was a knock and a bark at the back door. Dylan carried Trevor with him as he answered it. A huge black German shepherd bounded into the room and reared up on his hind legs, sniffing Trevor.

Welcoming the dog with one hand and holding the baby close enough for the dog to sniff, Dylan didn't seem alarmed. Nor did Trevor as he leaned down and plunged his sticky fingers into the dog's fur.

Dylan let Trevor touch the dog's head then held him back. "Come on, Sam. Down boy."

Sam? Black coat, four tan boots and a wisp of tan around the ears. This huge beast with all the teeth was the fur ball that Dylan had given her only a couple months before she left? The dog didn't seem to remember her, but he was certainly inquisitive about Tristan. Unsure of the dog, she stood and held her son as high as she could.

Dylan's cousin, whose name escaped her, stood just inside the door wearing jeans and a plaid western shirt, twisting his cowboy hat in his hands.

"He must have heard you drive in earlier because he's been whining and pacing for an hour stalking the back door for you to show up."

Dylan grinned. "Thanks for taking care of things around here. Any problems?"

"Had to mend the fence in the north pasture. Couple cows got out, but all accounted for. There's a fresh gallon of milk in the fridge and a loaf of bread I picked up in town this afternoon." He reached out and finger combed Trevor's blond curls. "Hey there, buddy."

"Trevor, this is your second cousin, Rusty." Dylan beamed like a proud father. "How much do I owe you for the groceries?"

Rusty, that was his name.

"Nothing. I took a package of corn out of your freezer and a jar of that mustang grape juice Mom made." He tousled Trevor's hair, moved past them and studied Tristan's face. "You're the spittin' image of your papa."

"His name is Tristan," Jordan interjected.

Sam stood on his hind legs, braced against Rusty's thigh for a closer look at Tristan, but Rusty secured the dog with one hand and tickled Tristan with the other. "You're excited to have new playmates, aren't you Sam?"

Tristan reached for the dog, almost putting his hand in the animal's mouth. But instead of biting, a long pink tongue lolled out and meticulously cleaned the applesauce off the tiny fingers in one sloppy swipe. Great, now Tristan would put that same hand in his mouth.

Rusty shook Tristan's sticky hand then finally looked at Jordan. "You probably don't remember me. Rusty Smith, Dylan's youngest cousin on his dad's side."

"Right. I'm Jordan, Dylan's—the mother of these two."

"Can't believe Dylan has two rug rats." He pushed Sam down and roughed up his fur, before turning his attention back to Dylan. "I'm headed to the Fort Worth stockyards tomorrow night, if you're interested."

Dylan shook his head, shifting Trevor's weight to the other arm. "Good luck. Don't go getting trampled by some pissed off bull."

"Yeah, well, they're all pissed off. That's what keeps things interesting." He gave Jordan a sideways glance, then nodded at Dylan's forearm, "Taken to wearing your food?"

Still holding his son, Dylan tore off a paper towel and dabbed at the green beans, then tossed it in the trash. "Not even my food."

Jordan hadn't heard a car drive up when Rusty arrived. "Do you live close by?"

"Rusty rents the old farmhouse and the south pasture from me. He's got some lame brain idea that he's going to be a professional bull rider."

"All around rodeo cowboy, like Uncle Mac," Rusty clarified.

"Well, you see where that got him." Dylan stood Trevor on the floor, right next to the huge dog.

Jordan fought for breath. "Don't do that!"

Sam barked and nudged the toddler with his snoot. Trevor plopped down hard on his diaper padded bottom. Jordan tried to grab her son, but still holding Tristan, couldn't move fast enough. Trevor clamped his mouth shut and turned his face away, but Sam continued cleaning food off Trevor's chubby little cheeks, one slobbery lick at a time.

"Get that dog away from him!"

Jordan struggled to balance Tristan while picking up Trevor, but Dylan grabbed him before she could wrangle him into her arms. "Sam won't hurt him. They have to get used to each other."

"I'd prefer a little more controlled introduction than just plopping my baby on the floor with a dog twice as big as he is and who doesn't know him." She closed her eyes and counted to ten. "Here, let me have him and I'll go clean them up."

"I'll carry him into the bedroom." Dylan held onto Trevor and narrowed his eye at Jordan. "Sam's used to my cousins' kids. And you're over-reacting."

Jordan wanted to object, but it was senseless. The boys had gotten too heavy for her to carry both of them at the same time anyway. Holding tight to Trevor, Dylan followed her into the bedroom. She sat Tristan on the bed. "I've got this. Just go visit with your cousin."

Dylan placed Trevor beside his brother. "I'll be back in a minute."

Whatever. As far as she was concerned, he could stay in the other room with Rusty for the remainder of the evening. She stripped both boys' soiled rompers off and led them into the bathroom where she could give Trevor his allergy meds. By the time she'd sponged them off, brushed their teeth and dressed them in their fuzzy blue pajamas, Dylan still hadn't returned. Good thing she didn't need his help. She handed the boys a stack of books out of their toy case and turned back the beds. They were fascinated by the horse motif on the sheets. She pointed one toddler toward each bed. "Climb in and look at your books. Pick one out for Mommy to read."

Trevor placed his books on the bed and hopped up like it was an adventure, but Tristan wasn't going for it. He made a beeline toward the door. Jordan caught him around the waist just before he escaped. But before she could close the door to keep him in, she heard Rusty.

"The boys are adorable, cuz. And I can see they've already got you wrapped. But you aren't going to let your love for them suck you back in with her, are you?"

"Not a chance. She's here so the boys won't be upset and to figure out how to share custody." Dylan's deep drawl came across loud and clear.

"Sorry, none of my business. But she's just not one of us, you know?" Rusty continued.

Jordan felt her heart thud to the floor. She wasn't sure why that stung since she had no desire for a relationship with Dylan McKeon, but it did.

She scooped Tristan up and closed the bedroom door, careful not to make even a click.

She plopped Tristan down on the unoccupied bed and handed him his favorite Dr. Seuss book. "Time to settle down."

Trevor grabbed a book about bunnies. "Book."

Tristan jumped down and without even looking at what he was picking up, chose a different book. "Mine!" He shoved the book at Jordan.

Dylan opened the door as Trevor started to cry. "Bunny ook."

Depositing Tristan beside his brother, Jordan sat between them with both books on her lap. Reading their bedtime story was her special time with them. "Tristan picked first last night so tonight we'll start with Trevor's bunny book."

"How about if I read to them?" Dylan asked

Chapter Five

Dylan raised an eyebrow as Jordan stared at him. "I like bunnies." She probably wouldn't appreciate him telling her how sexy she looked sitting there with a twin on each side and books piled around her.

"Not sure they're old enough for your kind of bunnies." She muttered under her breath then stood and handed him the books. "Fine."

Dylan grinned and took them, careful not to touch Jordan in the exchange. She sat on the far bed, wearing that no-nonsense expression of hers, as if she didn't believe he was capable of reading a bedtime story.

He sat on the bed with the twins and positioned a boy on each leg. "You guys like bunnies?"

They clapped. The book seemed pretty dull so Dylan adlibbed. "Look at that bunny. I bet he can hop really fast with those long legs."

Trevor leaned around and looked at him with a funny little frown, like he wasn't sure whether he'd lost his mind or didn't know how the story was supposed to go.

Dylan grinned. "Do you guys know how to hop?"

The twins bounded out of bed and started hopping across the floor like two fuzzy blue rabbits.

"You can't be real bunnies. You don't have ears." He held his hands up like ears and the boys copied the antic, continuing to hop. Oh yeah, this could be fun.

Trevor dug a worn out green bunny out of the toy case and presented it to him. "Bonbon."

Dylan took the half stuffed rabbit and hopped it across the bed. "Bonbon hops faster than you do."

"Dylan, they need to lie down and relax. This isn't play time." Jordan rubbed her eyes, then leveled her exasperated glare on him.

The woman had lost any ounce of spontaneity she'd ever possessed. But he patted the bed beside him, figuring this was the first night and he should try not to irritate her. "Come on, guys. Time to settle down." He picked up the second book and handed it to Tristan. "Why don't you read it to me?"

Tristan leaned back against Dylan's chest and opened the book. Dylan couldn't understand a word he said, but he pointed to each picture and obviously told the story and possibly added a few extra characters.

Trevor stuck his thumb in his mouth and looked slightly confused at his brother instead of Mommy reading their bedtime story. He crawled down and joined Jordan on the other bed, eying Dylan suspiciously.

Listening to Tristan babble, Dylan didn't try to coax Trevor back. They'd get used to him in time, hopefully. "Good job, Tristan."

A few more words of gibberish and Tristan slammed the book closed and tossed it on the floor. Dylan gave him a hug and placed him under the covers. He kissed his finger and touched it to the tiny mouth. "Love you. You have sweet dreams tonight, okay?"

Jordan kissed Trevor and tucked him under the covers in the other bed. "Good night, sweetie."

Without discussion, they exchanged places and each gave the other twin a good night kiss and hug. Trevor didn't object when Dylan hugged him, but as soon as he backed away, the boy reached his arms toward Jordan. "Mama."

She didn't hesitate, but returned to Trevor for a second hug. "Mommy's right here. I'm not going anyplace. Close your eyes."

Dylan felt something brush against his leg and caught Tristan as he raced by. "Where you going?"

The boy tried to pull away from Dylan and started crying, reaching for Jordan. "Mama!"

"It's fine. Just let him come over here."

She tucked them both into the same bed and softly started singing *Twinkle Twinkle Little Star*.

Dylan eased out of their line of vision and leaned against the door jamb, watching Jordan interact with them. He was still a bit in awe that these two little creatures were their children. It seemed surreal to suddenly have kids in the house, his kids.

They did their hands in the air along with Jordan in what he could only assume was supposed to simulate twinkling stars. The song couldn't possibly have as many verses as she sang. She repeated the lyrics five times before they finally drifted off to sleep. She whispered one more verse, then eased off the bed and put the pillow from the unused bed on the floor so that if Tristan rolled off, he'd land on the pillow. Trevor was against the wall so he had no place to roll.

She kissed the top of each boy's head and then joined Dylan in the doorway. He flipped the light out and everything was quiet for thirty seconds. Then all hell broke loose.

"Mama!" one of them screamed, but the other was too busy screaming at the top of his lungs to vocalize any particular words.

Jordan raced back into the room and flipped the light on. "It's okay. Mommy's here." She turned to Dylan. "They're accustomed to a night light."

Wow, one thing she hadn't packed. Where was he supposed to find a night light at ten o'clock on a Saturday night? "How about if I turn the bathroom light on and leave the door cracked open?"

The bathroom connected his bedroom to the twins' room. His mother called it a Jack and Jill bath. He switched the light on in the bathroom and looked at Jordan for her agreement that he should turn off the big light in the kids' room.

She nodded and then crowded into bed between them and pulled each against her side. "Close your eyes."

Dylan stood in the door as twice more Jordan got them to sleep, but both times as soon as she left the room, they started wailing. Sam sat straight up on full alert. Giving the door a dubious look, he stretched back out on the rug in front of the fireplace and put his paws beside his ears.

Dylan patted his head. "Right there with ya, boy."

He followed Jordan back into the room. Both boys rubbed their red eyes. He could relate.

Jordan sat and Trevor crawled into her lap. "This isn't working, Dylan."

Tristan jabbed at his eyes with his fists and wiped his nose on his pajamas' sleeve.

No kidding. "They aren't going to sleep in here without you and you can't all three get any sleep in that tiny bed. Let's take them into the guest room for tonight. Maybe if they play in here tomorrow they'll get accustomed to the room."

Jordan already held Trevor, but when he picked up Tristan, the boy reached for Jordan and acted like Dylan was the big bad boogie man. "Come on, son, I'm just carrying you to Mommy's room."

Tristan didn't take his eyes off Jordan as Dylan hauled him across the family room and held the door open for Jordan to precede him into the guest room. They placed the sniffling twins in bed. Jordan looked pretty much done in, but offered him a tired smile. "This is the best plan."

Good, because if things didn't quiet down, he'd get more sleep bunking in with Cinder in the barn. "You need anything?"

She shook her head. "We'll be fine. I know where things are if I do."

Dylan closed the door and before he realized what he was doing, had opened the fridge and reached for a beer. But there weren't any. There hadn't been since the night his father died. Dylan had come home from the hospital, scavenged the house and poured every last drop of alcohol down the drain.

He slammed the fridge. God, he needed a drink. Suddenly his dad's drinking every time Mom returned to California made more sense. But no way was a woman going to drive him to drink himself into an early grave.

Sam whined reminding Dylan that he hadn't fed him. Bending down, he buried his fingers in the thick coat and massaged Sam behind the ears. "You happy to be home?"

The dog's tongue lolled out and if dogs could smile, he did. He trotted behind, his nails clicking on the wood floor. Dylan poured fresh food into his dish and refilled his water bowl.

He rinsed out the kids' dishes and realized that with all the chaos, he and Jordan hadn't eaten dinner. He was too worked up to eat, but she might need a sandwich.

The noise from the bedroom had quieted. Maybe the boys were asleep. He should at least offer her something. He eased the door open to the guest room. The adjoining bathroom light was on and the door half open. Jordan was sound asleep in the center of the big bed, her dark auburn hair fanned across the pillow. Tristan was asleep with his little diaper clad bottom up in the air and his knees pulled up beneath him. Trevor was stretched out on Jordan's tummy with his head on her breast. Out like a light, but still sucking his thumb.

Sam nosed Dylan's hand and he ran his palm down the dog's soft snoot. "It's liable to be a long couple weeks, buddy."

* * *

Jordan had dressed the boys and fed them breakfast at the child-sized wooden table and chairs that had magically appeared in the kitchen overnight, and still no sign of

Dylan. Well, other than the note on the counter telling her to make herself at home.

The pickup was parked beside the house, but neither Dylan nor Sam had made an appearance. The dog was probably with Dylan, but wherever he was, at least he wasn't here. Not that she had anything against the dog. He'd been a sweet puppy and he was probably a nice enough dog, but the boys had never been around dogs. No telling what he'd do if they pulled his hair or spooked him.

She settled the boys with a tub of blocks on the large rug in front of the fireplace and cleaned up the kitchen. The kids were fine today in the daylight, but they'd woken up off and on all night. She'd pretty much heard the clock strike every hour.

"Tristan, back on the rug." She gave him a warning look and he turned away from the grandfather clock. Handing Tristan a couple blocks, she glanced at the photographs on the floor-to-ceiling shelf that flanked the fireplace. Mac riding a bull. Dylan suited up for high school football. Mac, Daisy, and Dylan standing in the surf. Grandparents and some other relatives Jordan hadn't met. Dylan boxing in the Army and another wearing a cowboy hat sitting astride Cinder.

She gently picked up one she'd placed there when they'd first moved here. She traced a finger over the ceramic palm tree on the frame, but her gaze stuck on the picture of her and Dylan in Florida. Both tanned and smiling, waves sparkling in the background. They weren't even the same people now.

She replaced the picture on the shelf and closed her eyes. Not a reminder she needed today.

And so the morning went. No sign of the man who so desperately wanted to be a father. The boys should be in daycare at home and she should be putting in her hours toward completing her internship. The only reason for being at this ranch was for the boys to get to know their father and he was MIA.

While the kids played, Jordan booted up her laptop, but she didn't have the key for the wireless. There was a computer in the study, but she was reluctant to turn it on. Maybe when Dylan came in, if he ever came in, he'd know the code so she could at least get her work done during the time she was here.

She fed the twins lunch and let them play in the bedroom where they were expected to sleep, in hopes that tonight wouldn't be a repeat of last night. To her amazement, with the help of some soft music, they both went down for naps. On a blanket on the floor with their toys and not in the beds, but at least in the appropriate room.

As she came out of the pantry with a can of soup for herself, Dylan walked in the back door. She froze as her gaze traveled slowly from his well-worn straw cowboy hat, to his unshaven jaw, dirty plaid shirt, jeans that fit his physique like, well, too tight to comment.

If it was true that clothes made the man, Dylan had it backwards. Nobody else in the world could fill out work clothes and have the effect on her that he did. Always had.

She remembered every inch of the body beneath that faded denim, and worse yet, he knew it. Knew what she was visualizing. She blinked and returned her gaze to his face, feeling her own face heat. "You spent lots of quality time with the boys this morning, huh?"

He tossed the cowboy hat on the hutch, went to the kitchen sink and washed his hands. A habit he well knew irritated her from when they'd lived together before. There was a sink in the laundry room. Sam continued to crunch his dry food, wisely keeping out of the line of fire.

Jordan tamped down her anger. "You aren't even going to talk to me? I put my entire life on hold so you could spend time with your sons."

Dylan grabbed a paper towel and dried his hands before turning to her. "Which I fully intend to do. But I've been working since five AM. I'm hungry and in no mood to get attacked when I walk in the door."

"Spoken like a typical father. Kids fall somewhere below the job on the priority scale."

"Spoken like a typical nagging wife. You planning to heat that soup or slurp it out of the can?" He flashed those deep dimples. "How about you share your soup and I'll make us a couple tuna sandwiches to go with it?"

She stared at the red and white can, befuddled that it was still in her hand. She reached under the cabinet for a pan and waited for him to speak, but he just busied himself making tuna salad.

"Dylan, seriously, what good is it for me and the twins to be here?"

"Give it a rest, Jordan."

She stirred a can of water into the soup and fumed. "After last night, you still think they'd be fine without me? What would you have done?"

"Probably plugged in a movie and let them play until they fell asleep."

She put her hand on her hip, but couldn't think of a rebuttal.

"Look, I wish I could spend all day with them, but I've got forty acres of hay that should have been bailed last week. If I don't get it in and sold, I don't have enough money to get through the winter. Animals have to be fed, just like kids."

"That's my point. You're busy. I'm the one taking care of the kids."

"If you're so bent out of shape about it, then go home. I'll hire someone for a couple days until Mom can wrap up her current project. Up to you, Jordan. You can leave anytime you want."

Tears sprung to her eyes. Exact same words he'd said to her the afternoon she'd left. They stung as much now as they had two years ago. But no way was she leaving her children here. Not even if his hippy dippy makeup artist mom was here to help.

* * *

Dylan stomped the dirt off his boots and rubbed the back of his hand across his forehead. He was whipped, but the last of the hay was bailed. And miraculously, the tractor hadn't died. He had to find some time and money to put his equipment back in shape. His equipment. Since his father had lost his long battle with liver disease, Dylan was no longer helping out around his dad's ranch, but instead making changes and attempting to make *his* ranch turn a profit. Well, his and Jordan's. One more item to add to the list of things they had to work out.

The sun had disappeared below the horizon half an hour ago. Tomorrow was soon enough to stack the hay he needed in the barn, and then with any luck the rancher who'd agreed to buy the remainder would come through.

Opening the back door, he had plans to read the boys a bedtime story, and then turn in. They'd been here three days and between the ranch and their early bedtime, he'd hardly squeezed in a half an hour a day with them.

The house was quiet and a light was on over the mantle, but nobody was in sight. He tossed his hat on the hutch and rubbed Sam's head. Even if Dylan was too tired to eat, the dog needed food.

Not bothering with the kitchen light, he poured food into Sam's bowl and then looked across the bar into the family room. Where was Jordan?

He should check on the boys. Sam padded along at his side into the kids' room. Toys were piled in their suitcase, but the beds were made. Since the twins had been playing and napping in here, he'd hoped they might feel comfortable enough to sleep here. He pushed his hair back. Maybe in a night or two, but they were still more at ease with their mom in touching range.

A shrill siren made him jump. He stooped down and picked up a toy fire truck hidden just under the edge of the spread.

Sitting on the bed, his mind struggled to grasp all the changes over the past three months. His father's death. Jordan owned half the ranch. Baby powder, toys, squished green beans. He stretched out. He was a father of two amazing little boys. What kind of arrangement could he and Jordan possibly come up with allowing them both to be a part of the kids' lives?

Jordan.

He closed his eyes to try to erase the image of her face, those incredible lips, but the vision only became more vivid. What the hell was he supposed to do about Jordan?

* * *

"Opn, opn, opn." Dylan flinched as something poked him in the eye. What the hell? He captured a tiny hand.

Tristan grinned. "Opn."

"They're open." Dylan squinted at the bright overhead light and tried to figure out where he was. What was he doing in the boys' room? "You're up early."

Grabbing the fire truck beside Dylan, Tristan presented it to him. "Brrrm."

What was that stench? Dylan sat up and squinted. He must have fallen asleep. He hadn't even taken off his boots. He frowned at Tristan. "You smell yucky, son."

"I forgot to take diapers into my room." Jordan fished a diaper out of the box and grabbed a tub of wet wipes. "You might want to crawl in your own bed. It's only three AM."

He yawned. "You need some help with that?" Jordan's baggy PJs, messy curls and sleepy eyes made her look like she could use a brotherly hug. So why did that turn him on?

"Well, since you're awake." Using two fingers, she held out a disgusting brownish diaper. At least she'd rolled it up so the worst of it was inside but the stench smelled worse than the outhouse at his grandparents' place when he was a kid.

"You might find a plastic bag for this while I clean him up and get him back to sleep."

Dylan stumbled into the kitchen, double bagged and tied the diaper in plastic grocery bags, then deposited it in the garage trashcan. He gulped down a glass of water then returned to the bedroom where Jordan was trying to corral four flailing appendages into a fresh fuzzy sleeper. "He doesn't look sleepy."

"Yeah, it may be a challenge." She zipped the sleeper and allowed Tristan to scramble off the bed.

He grabbed the fire truck on his way to Dylan. "Play."

Dylan could hardly see straight. Very little sleep the night before and then a long day. But his stomach was winning the battle over sleep. "How about you and Papa have a snack?"

Cocking her head, Jordan frowned. "You're going to reward him for waking up in the middle of the night?"

"Not his fault. If you had poopy britches, I bet you'd wake up too." The boy smelled like baby lotion and powder now. That explained why women used all that smelly stuff. "You like milk and cookies?"

While Dylan poured their milk, the clatter of Tristan pushing the truck across the stone kitchen floor made his head throb. "You want to join us?" he asked Jordan.

She leaned against the counter. "No thanks."

"You don't know what you're missing." He retrieved a box of wafers from the pantry and added it to the spread, then grabbed Tristan before he could push the truck any further.

Evidently the cookie was a fair trade for the truck as Tristan took the cookie out of his hand.

Dylan washed down a couple of cookies, then turned to Jordan. "They still won't sleep in their room?"

"It's not their room. They don't belong here." She closed her eyes. "I didn't mean that to come out like that."

Tristan held out his hand and Dylan placed a couple cookies on the bar for him. "Okay, so we change it up. The room needs to be Tristan and Trevor's."

Jordan sat down on the barstool beside him. "This is your house, not mine."

"But you know what would make them feel at home when they come for the summer or Christmas."

"I realize they'll be here sometimes, but..." Her chin jutted out and her expression turned hard. "I can't talk about this tonight. I'm going to bed. When you're done with your snack, just bring him in to me."

She got up and high tailed it to her room. Dylan shrugged at Tristan. "And I thought I was being accommodating? I hope you're better at understanding women than your old man is because I don't have a clue."

Chapter Six

Jordan was still agitated the next day when Dylan came in at lunch. There were too many memories in this house. Too many reminders of what she'd shared with Dylan, good and bad. For whatever reason, the small amount of time Dylan was around, Jordan was on edge. And that was new. Before, he'd been the one person she'd been totally at ease with.

He retrieved a loaf of bread from the pantry and plopped it on the cabinet then pulled a pack of lunchmeat from the fridge. "Where are the boys?"

"They didn't take a morning nap, so they're already down." Did he expect toddlers to adjust their schedules around any few minutes he might show up to see them?

She took a bowl from the cabinet and attempted to not focus on the way the soft flannel stretched across his shoulders as again, he washed his hands in the sink. One, two, three, four... "We need a few groceries and I don't have a vehicle."

She flinched as he plunked a set of keys on the counter. He bent his head and looked into her face. "The car seats are still in Dad's truck. But if you take my kids and run, I will come after you."

He hadn't followed when she'd left, but now that his kids were involved..."I would never do that."

"Pardon me if I'm not convinced." Those intense gray-green eyes sent icy shivers through her.

Okay, maybe she deserved that, but it wouldn't look good in court if she failed to hold up her end. "I will stay for two weeks as we agreed." She slipped the keys into her pocket and changed the subject. "I'll run into town when they wake up."

He backed off. "If you want to wait until I'm done, we can all go tonight or one of us can stay home with the kids. Whatever is easiest."

"I'm used to handling them." His closeness had her heart pounding, but she wasn't about to be the first to look away.

He tossed a couple bills on the counter and fished his ringing cell phone out of his pocket. "Dylan." He grabbed a bottle of water from the fridge. "Not catching me at a bad time."

Jordan removed the soup from the burner and tried not to be affected by Dylan's smile. It wasn't a huge, forced smile, but relaxed and comfortable.

"Who does he belong to?" Dylan asked the caller as he wrapped the sandwich in a paper napkin and placed it and the bottle into his hat. Cradling the hat in one arm like a basket, he held the phone with the other hand. "Sure, bring him on."

Dylan clicked the phone off and stuck it into his pocket and turned to Jordan. "Don't wait dinner tonight." He motioned to the dog. "Come on boy. Ready to move some cows?"

Without waiting for her response, he took off out the back door with Sam dogging his heels.

"Fine." She glanced at the grocery money he'd left on the counter. "Just-fine."

* * *

The wheels crunched as Jordan whipped the pickup onto the white rock road to the ranch. Amazing how quickly driving the huge crew cab truck had come back to her. Okay, so she'd found a parking place far out in the lot so she could pull forward and not have to back the monster, but she'd managed.

The trip had been a nice breather from the ranch. Dylan's black cows were grazing peacefully in the opposite pasture from when she'd left. The pasture with the stock tank where she and Dylan had lazed away a Sunday afternoon a couple years ago. Dylan had baited the hooks and stuck two cane poles into the tank dam as if to justify that they were there to fish. Yet they'd stretched out on an old blanket beside the water and... She blinked, trying to erase the memory.

Tristan's jabbering jarred her back to reality. She parked beside the garage to make it easier to carry the twins and the groceries in. The boys had been well behaved, given that they were at the age where they wanted everything they saw. She squinted into the sun. Whose red pickup and horse trailer was beside the stable?

Gently she unbuckled Tristan from his seat and stood him on the drive, then unbuckled Trevor. Shouldering her purse and grabbing a bag of groceries, she headed toward the house with the twins trotting along behind. Early November and it was eighty degrees. Last week, Connecticut had snow on the ground.

She plugged the twins new video into the DVD player, wiped Trevor's nose and parked them in front of the TV long enough to haul in groceries. Tristan dumped the plastic bin of Legos in the center of the rug and Trevor grabbed for his share.

At least Dylan hadn't complained when she'd put away the things that could hurt them or that they could break. At her parents' house everything was expensive and breakable and the world would end if anything moved from its designated spot.

She loaded her arms with grocery bags then stopped as a loud banging sounded from the direction of the trailer. A spotted horse lunged out of the trailer and raced in circles around the round pen. The animal looked like it could use a good meal. Jordan shifted the groceries and had started toward the house when she caught sight of a leggy redhead beside Dylan. He'd closed the gate and the two of them were standing hip to hip as they watched the horse.

She was tall, like Dylan. Both lean and fit. A curly red ponytail stuck out the back of the woman's baseball cap.

"Here, let me help you with those." Jordan jumped as Dylan's cousin grabbed the remaining bags of groceries from the truck bed. How did he sneak up on her without her hearing him?

"Thanks, Rusty." At the sound of laughter, Jordan glanced back at the red pickup. Head tossed back, the redhead nudged Dylan with her shoulder and he joined in her laughter.

"Zoe's the best damn vet we've had since old man Johnson retired. Impressive, isn't she?"

Zoe? Jordan led the way into the house, dug a stalk of bananas out of the bag and peeled one for the boys. Breaking it in half, she walked over to give each boy their snack. Trevor grabbed his half, but Tristan continued masterminding the Lego creation he was working on. "Tristan, here's your banana."

He didn't even look up.

Fine. She took a bite of the banana and returned to the kitchen where Rusty had started putting away the groceries. What was he doing up here when Dylan could certainly use his help in the stable?

Rusty retrieved a cold soda from the fridge. "You mind?"

"Go ahead." She figured he and Dylan had worked out whatever the arrangement regarding food and each other's houses. "Did Dylan buy a new horse?"

Rusty popped the top on the soda. "Some moron on the other side of town evidently found him a little too high spirited and took a whip to him. Zoe don't take too kindly to that crap."

Jordan glanced out the window at Zoe and Dylan standing beside the pickup. "So she rescued him? The horse, I mean."

Rusty drained the soda. "She and Dylan are good together. Zoe heals the physical scars and Dylan re-socializes them." The horse bucked and then continued to circle the pen. "He's a bit skittish. They'll bring him around though." Rusty ruffled each twin's hair before ambling back toward the stable.

Good together? Dylan was a man. It had been over two years since he and Jordan had split. But...

Jordan peeped through the blind slats as Dylan opened the pickup door and Zoe slid in. He closed the door but kept his hands on the open window. In the process, he shifted so his back was to Jordan and she couldn't see whether he touched the woman's face or possibly leaned in far enough for a kiss.

She swallowed the last bite of banana just as Trevor tugged on her pants leg. "Nana."

Jordan peeled another banana and handed him half. But the truck still hadn't passed down the white rock road beside the house headed toward the highway.

Her stomach felt sick imagining Dylan with the leggy redhead and how well the two of them would fit together. *Erase that image.* She certainly didn't have to stand here and witness their little whatever. Still, what were they talking about so intently? Jordan let the slat fall back into place.

Possibly now that Dylan had two kids in the house, they were planning when and where they might hook up next?

* * *

Best of intentions didn't exactly work out as Dylan had planned. The rescue horse, Paint, had to be settled in. Which caused Cinder to demand a little extra attention. So once again, the sun had set before Dylan made his way to the house.

He found Jordan sitting cross-legged on the sofa, tapping away on her laptop. The way she was sitting on the overstuffed sofa, she looked too young to be a mom.

"Boys already asleep?"

Gently, Jordan snapped the laptop closed. "I usually put them down between eight and eight-thirty."

Meaning, he should have come in an hour ago. He was too tired to fight. "Sorry. I really did plan to get in early enough to see them tonight."

She placed the laptop on the end table and folded her hands. "And I'm sorry about my attitude. I do realize ranch life is demanding."

He sat down on the hearth and faced her. God she was pretty when she was like this. Sweet, almost innocent. "Jordan, I appreciate that you've put your life on hold. Tomorrow, I'll spend part of the day with the boys. Maybe feed them breakfast."

"Okay." She nodded. "They're enjoying eating at the little table you brought in. It makes them feel big."

"Grandpa McKeon built it when I was a boy. He'd be tickled that my kids are getting some use out of it too."

Her mouth turned up at the corners, just a smidge. Face scrubbed free of makeup and wearing a pair of sweats and tee shirt, she wasn't exactly going for sexy, but he remembered how many times he'd seen her that way. Not the polished, shorter haircut, face-painted persona she was striving for these days. It had taken him weeks to convince her that she didn't have to make herself up for him. He preferred her natural beauty.

"I take it the trip into town went off without a hitch?"

"It was nice to get out." Jordan shrugged. "Saw you got a new horse."

He tried to decipher the reason for her mood change. "He's a rescue horse. I'll work with him, socialize him and Zoe will find him a new home."

"Zoe is attractive," Jordan said.

Nothing to be gained by denying the obvious. "She is that."

"She's a veterinarian?"

"Best large animal vet around. Nice lady, but I feel for the guy who owns that horse by the time that red-headed temper of hers is done with him."

Jordan twisted a strand of hair around her finger and didn't respond for a few minutes. "So you two are friends?"

Was that jealousy? "Yep."

The grandfather clock ticking echoed. Dylan tucked a stray strand of hair behind Jordan's ear. God, those flecks of green in her golden brown eyes always did him in. "Being under the same roof is a little uncomfortable for us both."

Their gazes locked for a second in the dim light before she bolted to her feet. "Um, there's some leftover chicken and potatoes in the fridge. But ahh, I think I'll call it a night."

He squelched the urge to grin at her nervousness. "G'night."

* * *

While he was feeding the animals the next morning, Dylan realized he'd left his cell phone at the house. When he finished here, he'd swing by and grab it before he got knee deep in manure mucking out the stalls. With the twins here, he didn't want to be out of pocket. Trevor still had allergies, or in his opinion a good old fashioned cold. Hopefully he could feed them breakfast while he was there.

It was before eight, but the kids were up, dressed, and evidently fed. Jordan sat perched on one of the barstools. She looked up from her laptop and frowned. "Your phone's been ringing for thirty minutes."

Well pardon me for forgetting it. What happened to her understanding mood from the night before? He swiped the phone off the bar and looked at the read out. Punching the missed call button, he made his way into the living room to say good morning to the boys while waiting for Zoe to answer. "Hey guys."

Dylan squatted down and Tristan handed him the tractor he'd become attached to. Trevor sucked his thumb, engrossed in the big yellow bird on TV.

Tristan turned the tiny steering wheel. "Ook."

"Cool. You can help Papa plow when you're bigger."

Zoe answered the phone and Dylan continued to watch Tristan push the tractor. "Good morning."

"How's our horse today? When you didn't answer, I thought maybe I should come by and check to make sure he hadn't knocked you on your ass."

Dylan grinned. "He still isn't happy, but I put him out in the small pasture for the day. He waited until I turned my back to eat, but that's par."

"Yeah. I've got a couple stops this morning, but I'll try to swing by this afternoon and see about that wound on his flank."

Jordan strolled into the room, picking up toys and straightening the kids' blankets. She didn't even look at Dylan.

"Okay," he said to Zoe. "I've got stuff to get to also. Later."

Jordan didn't even wait until he got the phone in his pocket. "So I guess that means you aren't planning to spend time with the boys today either?"

Everything he did or said led to a fight. "Are we going to do this again?"

"You're right. Why bother? Nothing changes anyway." She folded and smoothed every crease out of the blue blanket Trevor always lugged around.

These prissy moods of hers infuriated him. "Hey, I tell you what. You own half the ranch, how about you squeeze that cute little ass of yours into a pair of jeans and muck the stalls. I'll spend the morning with my boys."

Placing the blanket on the end of the sofa, she sized him up. "Okay." Her eyes blinked as if she was still registering what she'd just agreed to. "That's just...fine."

Trevor never looked up, but Dylan and Tristan both watched Jordan depart into the bedroom. As soon as Dylan sat down on the sofa, Sam stretched out in front of the hearth on the Navajo rug, as if realizing he had the morning off.

When he'd first moved back here with Jordan to take care of his father after the car accident, she'd sometimes helped Dylan with chores. Other than in bed, it was the only time they'd had alone. She knew the basic task, but he couldn't imagine her actually managing all eight stalls.

Jordan returned wearing tight jeans, sneakers, and a black tee shirt. She hugged each boy. "See you guys in a few hours. Have fun with Papa." She glanced at Dylan. "Trevor's had his allergy meds. He can't have another dose until after eleven."

Trevor's little lip dropped down as she walked away, but he didn't cry. Tristan followed her to the back door and peered out the side window. Dylan waited until he returned. The boy looked at him through teary eyes, bottom lip pouting.

Dylan ruffled his hair and scooped him into his arms. "Looks like we're on our own, guys.

Chapter Seven

Jordan hadn't even had time to make it to the barn before the twins took off in opposite directions. Tristan ran for the bedroom and by the time Dylan caught him and returned, Trevor had vanished.

With Tristan under one arm, Dylan tracked Trevor to the kitchen pantry. Standing on tiptoe on the little step stool used to reach things on the top shelf, he'd already snagged a box of raisins.

Dylan grabbed another box and deposited both boys in their playroom. Tristan ate a few raisins but mostly tossed toys out of the suitcase while Trevor sat on Dylan's leg and shared his raisins.

The room seemed safe and the raisins had made him thirsty. "Boys, Papa is going to the kitchen. You stay here and play. Okay?" Neither one even looked his way, but Tristan nodded. Evidently the best answer he was going to get.

The coffee pot was still hot so he poured a cup and grabbed two juice boxes for the kids. Sam followed him to the playroom and stretched out to guard the door.

Dylan poked the straws into the boxes for the twins and sat on one of the beds while they raced around as if they had a purpose. Just watching them made him tired.

Tristan gravitated toward anything with wheels, but Trevor went for stuffed animals and books about animals. He'd have to take them for a horseback ride before they left.

Using the large Lego blocks, Dylan built a path for Tristan to drive his cars down. Hopefully he'd get better at staying between the lines before he hit his teens or driving was going to be an expensive endeavor. When they were older, he'd teach them to drive the tractor and the pickup. Not much to run into in the pasture. Dylan grinned, remembering when he was sixteen and got the pickup stuck trying to cross the creek running through the property. That hadn't gone over well with his dad and he seemed to recall the girl riding with him at the time hadn't appreciated his driving either.

Trevor wanted a bed for his stuffed dog so Dylan adlibbed on how to accomplish that. It ended up looking like a multi-colored rectangle, but it seemed to please Trevor as he stuffed the dog in and told it, "Night night."

Tristan handed Dylan a green Lego and held a similar red device to his tiny ear. "Hello."

Dylan raised the green Lego to his own ear. "Hello, Tristan. Did you get a new phone?"

Nodding, Tristan started pacing in a circle, jabbering into his makeshift phone. Dylan tried not to laugh at how the kid had picked up Jordan's pacing habit.

A really strong odor wafted up as Tristan got closer. "Great. You need clean britches, son."

The kid wrinkled up his little nose and nodded, still talking into the phone. "Ucky."

Dylan grabbed a diaper and a tub of wet wipes and coaxed him to lie down. The diaper was even worse than the one from the other night. Dylan put one leg across the kid's chest to keep him from crawling away before he could get him clean. But as soon as he moved his leg, Tristan rolled over and crawled out of reach. His little bare bottom wiggled back and forth as he laughed and raced into the other room.

Dylan carried the dirty diaper into the kitchen to tie it up in a plastic bag. He let Tristan run naked long enough to get the diaper into the garage trash then wrangled him back into the play room for a clean one. By then Trevor smelled worse and his outfit was soiled. "Twice the fun huh! You guys are old enough to learn to use the potty."

As he sacked Trevor into clean clothes, his stomach growled. Hauling one giggling boy under each arm, he wondered what they'd eat. There was an assortment of canned vegetables in the pantry. He left them in the microwave too long and had to wait for them to cool. Tristan didn't mind, but he almost tripped over Trevor who stayed right under his feet. "Go sit at your table."

Lunch wasn't bad, until he turned from loading the dishwasher and found Tristan standing on his chair. "Sit down!"

Tristan's lip quivered and he started crying. Hearing his brother, Trevor followed suit. Dylan gave up on the dishes and took the twins back to their room to clean them up. His stomach could wait.

But they wouldn't stop crying and Trevor kept wailing, "Mamamama!"

"Papa's going to have to do for now, guys." Trevor wrapped his arms around Dylan, screeching in his ear.

He scooped Tristan up and hugged both of them. "I'm not such a bad guy, am I? You're big boys. We can do this."

He fished a chunk of carrot out of Trevor's blond hair. "How about a bath? You like baths?"

The wails magically turned to babbling. Trevor stripped off his own diaper while Dylan undressed Tristan. Trevor started tossing bath toys into the tub from the basket. He hadn't realized bath time was such a big deal. Careful not to get soap in their eyes, he soaped and rinsed them, then tried to coax them out of the tub. They weren't happy but he finally managed to dress them and started picking up the bath toys.

He added his dripping shirt to the pile of baby clothes. Jordan would think he was incompetent if she saw this mess. He should start a load of laundry, but it could wait. He didn't have that much time with the boys.

Jordan still hadn't returned by one o'clock. Maybe he should call her cell. No way. She got the easier job out of this deal, probably didn't even smell as bad as the twins.

It was past time for their nap. Dylan told them good-night, laid them down, and covered them up, but as soon as he left the room, they screamed. They'd been napping in here, so what was the problem? Every time he even hinted they should close their eyes, they pitched fits.

Forget it. He gave up and spread a blanket on the living room floor. Hopefully their new movie would hold their attention.

They played while he made himself a sandwich and sat down at the bar, keeping the twins in sight. Whatever they were talking about, they seemed to understand each other. Happy as clams as long as they were getting their way.

At least they were engrossed in the movie, even if they were still playing. He stretched out on the sofa and enjoyed watching them. Tristan resembled his own baby pictures, but Trevor was fairer. His face was oval with a point to his chin that became more pronounced when he didn't get his way, exactly like Jordan.

Trevor had just finished stacking four Lego's on top of each other when Tristan snatched the top one for his project. Trevor squealed and kicked the remaining blocks across the floor and then crawled up on the couch with Dylan. He slipped his arm around the boy as he stretched out on his chest, reveling in the acceptance. Within minutes

Trevor was asleep sucking his thumb and clutching a handful of Dylan's hair in the other fist.

Once he'd won the prized Lego, Tristan lost interest and stretched out watching the video. He didn't move for at least ten minutes. Had to be asleep. Hopefully anyway, as Dylan was done in. They hadn't been calm at the same time all day. Maybe if he was really quiet...

* * *

Jordan could feel the wind shift to the north and sand stung her cheeks as it blew across the corral. A dark purple bank of clouds churned on the northern horizon and the horses raced around the pasture, tails high and flying. She couldn't wait to get inside and clean up. Dirt and horse poop caked her jeans. Her French manicure was history. She'd sweated out her shirt and probably smelled like one of the horses.

She stomped dirt off her boots, then pushed the back door open. Not the best day she'd ever had, but the stalls were done and she hadn't quit until she was sure they were perfect.

She blinked. The house looked like the scene from a disaster movie. Tristan and Sam were stretched out asleep among a pile of Legos in front of the fireplace. Trevor had fallen asleep on his sleeping Papa's chest.

She sucked in her breath. *Bare* chest.

Dylan's bare chest...

Jordan's body reacted in primal feminine fashion. Had it really been two years? Her son sleeping peacefully against that chest sucked the air from her lungs.

There were dirty dishes on the counter, soiled clothes in the doorway of the kids' room, toys scattered everywhere, and the TV blaring with nobody watching. But all she felt was a sense of belonging, of being home.

Dylan turned his head and flashed a sleepy grin. "Hey. You survived."

She tried to swallow past the lump in her throat. "What happened here?"

Looking slightly sheepish, he whispered. "Twins?"

She couldn't let this feeling draw her in. It wouldn't last. She shoved a strand of sweaty hair off her face. "Did you let them run completely undisciplined?"

His grin dropped. "Yeah." He rubbed Trevor's back and adjusted his position so he didn't tumble onto the floor.

"Why aren't they in their beds?"

"Because they cry."

Jordan gritted her teeth and started to pick Tristan up off the blanket, then remembered she was filthy from mucking stalls. "I'm going to grab a quick shower."

"Good plan." Dylan wrinkled his nose, but she caught that hint of a grin.

She quickly showered, brushed her wet hair back and pulled on her comfy gray sweats. Hauling her stinky clothes out with her, she headed toward the pile of kids' laundry by their door.

Dylan had put the boys in the twin beds and she was relieved to find that he'd also put on a shirt. He was busy tying up dirty diapers in a plastic bag. "Aren't they old enough to potty train?"

She scooped up the dirty clothes. "Boys mature slower than girls. I'm waiting until they're two."

"My vote is to start yesterday." He tossed a couple stuffed animals back into the open case they were using as a toy box. "I mean, seriously. Keeping one kid changed is bad enough, but I no more than got one clean then the other smelled worse. It's like they've each got to one up the other. 'Hey, bro you stink. But get a whiff of this.'"

Jordan shook her head. "You work around horse poop every day and you're complaining about a couple stinky diapers?"

He stopped, still holding an armful of toys. "Horse poop? You still can't say horse shit?"

"Whatever you call it, it stinks."

"Well, yeah." He dumped the armful of toys. "But taking care of horses doesn't involve diapers."

He had a point. Not that she particularly enjoyed mucking stalls, but at least she did it with a shovel, not her bare hands. Lugging her dirty clothes into the laundry room, she tried to figure out the fancy washer.

The first time around, laundry had been one of Dylan's chores. After his mom had moved back to California, he and his father had been on their own.

Dylan was in the kitchen by the time she started the washer. "I took some vegetable soup out of the freezer."

The guy was more domestic than she was. *He*'d taught *her* to cook. Jordan's mouth watered just remembering all the wonderful food that made its way straight from the McKeon family garden into the freezer. When his grandmother was alive, she and Dylan's two aunts had 'put up' vegetables and soups until you couldn't fit one more package into the huge freezer. Mac and Dylan had worked the garden and the women did the canning. An experience she'd never forget.

Dylan fished his ringing phone from his pocket while he pulled a pan from the cabinet. "Dylan."

His face melted into a warm grin. "Sure. I've got to go put them back in the stable. That cold front is already moving in." He sat the pan on the stove. "That works."

He turned back to Jordan. "I won't be long."

"Okay."

He stuffed his feet into his boots, grabbed a denim jacket off the hook beside the back door and was gone before she could blink. Zoe was obviously on the way.

None of my business.

She got the soup on to heat and the cornbread mixed before Tristan trotted in for a hug. There was no more magical feeling in the world than those tiny arms around her neck, and she needed that right now. She carried him in to change his diaper and Trevor woke up. They followed her back into the living room, already adjusted to the routine of the house. If they wanted to play in the middle of the living room, that's where they played. Not once had they been allowed to do that at her parents' house, but in no time, they'd grown accustomed to having the freedom to be part of their surroundings.

The rustic style of the house didn't suit her taste, but it was built for a family. She could stir the soup at the bar while keeping an eye on the boys playing in front of the hearth.

She looked up as Zoe's red pickup passed the window. The woman was a vet. Maybe she just stopped by to check on the horse. And even if there was more...

Jordan had just put the cornbread in the oven when the back door opened. Cold air rushed in as Dylan stood aside for the redhead to enter. The temperature was falling, or was it Jordan's mood?

"Zoe, this is Jordan." Dylan looked a little cautious. "Jordan, Zoe."

The dog trotted past in route to his food bowl, oblivious to everyone's discomfort.

"Hello." Jordan rubbed her hands down the front of her dull gray sweatpants, conscious of the other woman's jeans that clung to her long legs like a second skin.

"Hi. Hope I'm not interrupting dinner. I just have a minute," Zoe offered.

The twins found their visitor more interesting than the TV program. But at least they stopped behind Jordan's legs to check out Zoe from a distance.

Zoe knelt and held out two little cowboy hats. They weren't the bright red kiddy hats either. One was brown felt and the other black and they looked like the real deal. She was obviously trying to score points with the kids.

They were her kids, yet Jordan felt like odd man out.

Trevor stepped right up to Zoe, reaching for the brown hat.

Zoe placed it on his blond curls. "Your Papa told me all about you. You must be Trevor. The girls will never know what hit them when you turn sixteen."

Staring up at his papa's hat, he caressed the felt like it was the most awesome gift he'd ever received. Jordan's sweet, cuddly Trevor who always took a long time to warm up to strangers had walked up to this woman as if they were old friends.

Jordan's stomach felt queasy.

Zoe looked quizzically at the black hat. "I wonder if there is someone else here who needs a hat."

"Me." Tristan darted out from behind Jordan and reached for the remaining hat.

Placing it on his head, Zoe adjusted it slightly to the back. "Hi Tristan. Wow, you're a good looking little man too. The daddies around here had better lock up their daughters when you get a little older."

Jordan clenched her fists.

Tristan touched Zoe's mass of red curls in awe. "Oooo."

Jordan caught the grin on Dylan's face. "Pretty, huh son?"

Jordan's wanted to snatch up her boys and kick the other woman out. If Dylan married Zoe, she'd be spending time with Jordan's kids. Zoe might even want to start a family. Jordan fought to keep her expression impassive. One reason not to sign the ranch over to Dylan. She had to protect Tristan and Trevor's interest. If everything happened for a reason, maybe, even if the older man hadn't realized what it was, there was a higher power behind Mac's putting half the ranch in Jordan's name.

Standing, Zoe extended her hand to Jordan. "It's nice to meet you. Your boys are amazing."

"Thank you." Jordan hesitated. She wanted to hate the other woman. She was dangerously attractive. Couldn't she have had acne or buck teeth? *Hold the enemy close.* "There's plenty if you'd like to stay for dinner."

Glancing at Dylan, Zoe studied his face then shook her head. "I really have to get going, but thanks. Maybe another time."

"I'll walk you out," Dylan offered.

Zoe said goodbye to the kids and preceded Dylan out the door. For once, the dog didn't follow. Must not like the worsening weather conditions. Jordan turned on the overhead light to brighten the darkening room as storm clouds rolled in.

She tried not to watch out the window, but like a horrific wreck, she couldn't look away.

Chapter Eight

"What do you mean?" Dylan pulled the front of his jacket together and narrowed his eyes at Zoe.

Turning toward the wind, she let it whisk her hair back. "I mean that before we go any further down this road, you need to figure out what's going on inside that house. Jordan was cordial, but if looks could kill, I'd be six feet under."

He closed his eyes. "It's over between her and me. Has been for two years."

"Really?" She held her hair back from her face.

He'd met Zoe almost a year ago when she'd moved here. They'd only recently progressed beyond friendship. He wasn't sure what he was supposed to say. "I don't know. The twins complicate things."

"I'm not going anywhere, Dylan. But if you decide to come to me, I have to be sure that it's me you want." Reaching out to straighten his collar, she looked him in the eye. "Okay?"

"Yeah." If he could trust any woman to stick to her word and not desert him, it was Zoe. But then he'd thought the same about Jordan.

Zoe touched his face. "If Jordan doesn't realize what she's got now, she will. She'd be foolish not to."

He could argue that point from a couple angles, but to what end? They weren't together and he had doubts whether he even wanted to go there again. The one thing he demanded in a relationship was commitment and Jordan had already proven that was not in her genes.

Pulling Zoe gently into his arms, he held her warm body against his. "Anybody ever tell you you're too nice for your own good?"

She ran a hand up his chest then wrapped her arms around his neck and returned the hug. "You just haven't seen my bad side," she said, backing away from the embrace.

He opened her pickup door and steadied her arm as she stepped in. He wasn't sure whether he'd ever get his life together regarding Jordan and the twins, but until he did, it wasn't fair to drag Zoe into this. Even though he might lose Zoe as a lover, he wasn't willing to lose her as a friend. "I have no intention of getting on your bad side. I'm not stupid."

"Never stupid. A little naïve maybe." She grinned and finger combed his hair out of his eyes. "You better get inside out of this weather."

He pushed off from the truck. "Drive safe."

Dylan snapped his jacket as he watched the tail lights of Zoe's pickup fade. Her taking the step to back away from things was actually a relief. He would have done it himself, but she'd made it easy for him.

Typical Zoe. Approached life more like a guy. Could be because she'd grown up with three brothers. Logical, no nonsense, a straight shooter. But man could she get worked up.

Unlike Jordan who used her logic to disguise an insecure emotional wreck. Problem was that she'd fallen for her own hype. He'd thought the year they were together that she'd learned to make better choices by dealing with her emotions instead of ignoring them. But evidently she'd returned to Hartford and fallen right back under her father's emotions-make-you-weak mantra.

Dylan turned his collar up. Raindrops plopped in little dots on the drive. He inhaled the fresh smell of rain and damp soil. The cold front had arrived with a vengeance and judging by the low hanging clouds, if he didn't get that wood in now, he was going to get drenched.

He gathered an armload of logs and tromped the sticky damp dirt off his boots before opening the door. A fire would feel good tonight.

Jordan glanced up, but continued to stir the soup in silence. He hadn't known how to introduce the two women, but Zoe had asked to meet the boys and he'd wanted her to. If Jordan chose to pout, that was her choice.

Tristan and Trevor bounced up and down in excitement watching him build the fire and retrieve the fireplace tools out of the closet. He made them stand back and stuffed some old newspapers in with the kindling in order to get the flame going.

"Ooooo," Trevor said edging closer to the bright flames.

"It's hot. Don't get too close." Dylan squatted down and wrapped an arm around each toddler. "Stand here with me."

Sam stretched out on the rug in front of the fire, staking out his territory.

Trevor plopped down on Dylan's knee, but daredevil Tristan leaned forward for a closer look. "Hot."

"Very hot." He tightened his arm on Tristan. "After dinner we'll have popcorn."

Tristan's eyes sparkled. Trevor was too busy staring into the fire to even react.

* * *

After they finished eating, Dylan shooed Jordan away. "I'll clean up. You cooked."

She nodded at the mess around the twins' little table. "Cool. I'd rather bathe kids than scrub that table."

Smushed vegetables and spilled soup dripped off the edge onto the chairs. This might involve scrubbing down every inch of the table and chairs. He fished a quarter out of his pocket. "I'll flip you for it."

"Uh uh. You already volunteered for KP duty." Jordan took each boy by the hand. "Bath time, kiddos."

Dylan cleaned up, turned on the coffee pot then went out to the shed for more firewood. In the corner, he caught site of the old wooden rocking horse his grandfather had built for him. God, he'd spent many an hour on that thing. His parents were a bit unorthodox in their parenting style, but his grandparents had been A-one.

The boys should get a kick out of the rocking horse. He wiped it down and sat it in front of the fireplace. He kicked off his boots and took a seat in the recliner. The heat felt good. With any luck, maybe he and Jordan could get through the evening without arguing.

Lightning flashed through the room as rain pattered against the windows and thunder rolled across the fields. The first 'Norther' of the season always made him want to stay inside and hunker down. The fire crackled and Dylan inhaled the mesquite smoke as he watched to make sure none of the sparks came through the screen.

The mesquite popped, but Sam didn't even flinch as he rolled over with all four feet up in the air. "You've got a dog's life there, buddy."

Trevor raced into the room three steps ahead of his brother and was the first to spot the rocking horse. "Horsey!"

Sitting up, Dylan held it steady for him to climb on. "Hold on." After placing Trevor's little hands on the handles, Dylan gently rocked the horse. "Can you do it yourself?"

Trevor bounced up and down, but didn't grasp the concept of back and forth. Dylan tried to move his body, but the kid was so excited, he couldn't stop bouncing.

"Me," Tristan demanded.

"Just a minute. Let your brother finish his turn, then you can try. Where's your new cowboy hat?"

Jordan sat on the hearth and reached for Tristan, but he raced into the kitchen and returned wearing the black hat, not wanting to risk missing his turn. "You only have one? This isn't going to work."

"Sorry, my grandfather didn't know I was going to have twins when he made it." If she always bought two of everything, they'd be spoiled rotten. "They can share. It won't kill 'em to take turns."

Trevor wasn't happy when Dylan lifted him off and Tristan climbed on, taking to the rhythm of rocking like second nature. "Come on, Trev, let's see if Sam wants to play. Sam, get your ball."

Sam rolled to his feet looking none too thrilled with having his nap interrupted.

"Get your ball."

Sam sniffed his way around the sofa and returned with his red ball. Dylan took it and handed it to Trevor. "Throw it toward the kitchen."

Trevor tossed the ball, but it landed on the sofa. Sam bounded up, snagged the ball and brought it back. "Good boy." Dylan took it out of his mouth and handed it back to Trevor. "Try again."

Trevor erupted into giggles as the dog raced after the ball, then returned and dropped it at his feet. After a couple rounds, Dylan headed toward the kitchen. "Weren't we going to make popcorn?"

Trevor trotted along beside him, glancing over his shoulder every other step to watch his brother. Dylan stuck a bag of popcorn in the microwave and filled the boys' sippy cups with milk. "Take this one to Mommy for Tristan." Dylan handed him one cup. He poured two cups of coffee for him and Jordan and then handed Trevor his own milk. Dumping the popcorn into a plastic bowl, he kept an eye on the boys as Jordan coaxed Tristan off the rocking horse by handing him Sam's ball to throw.

Dylan handed Jordan her coffee, placed his on the mantle and set the popcorn on the raised brick hearth.

Trevor's interest was torn between racing for the rocking horse and food.

Jordan took a sip of coffee, then a handful of popcorn. "Come here, Trevor. Want a bite?"

Deciding the popcorn was more interesting, Tristan dropped Sam's ball and plopped down on the hearth beside the bowl.

Dylan ate a couple handfuls while watching the twins run in circles, dropping popcorn as they ate. Sam followed behind, cleaning up after them. "The rain's coming down in sheets."

Jordan nodded, up-righting Trevor's sippy cup.

The kids slowed and their eyes looked droopy, especially Trevor's, so he figured maybe they'd quiet down soon and go to sleep. One more turn each on the rocking horse and Dylan moved it behind the sofa while Jordan pulled a couple books off the shelf. Trevor was fine with that, but ever the rebel, Tristan took off around the sofa. Dylan snagged him and tossed him over his head. "Where you going, pal?" He placed him on the rug and started tickling him.

Tristan giggled, trying to wiggle out of his grasp. Trevor left Jordan and inched closer so Dylan tossed him beside his brother and tickled them both.

Trevor had a funny little giggle. Out of the corner of his eye, Dylan saw Jordan sitting to the side, looking slightly perturbed.

He rolled over and the boys crawled on top and started tickling him. He laughed, delighted with how cute they were when they were all wound up.

Jordan frowned, leaned against the sofa and rested the book in her lap. "Time to settle down and read our bedtime story."

No way. She needed to be part of the fun, not just the Mommy who read them a book every evening at precisely 8:15. "Hey, guys. Mommy needs tickling."

Both boys pounced, tiny fingers wiggling before they even reached her. "Gitchy gitchy," Trevor said, burying his fingers in Jordan's belly.

She smiled tolerantly at the kids, but she wasn't laughing. And she needed to laugh. For the twins' sake. For her sake. "Here, let Papa help." He grabbed her around the waist and rolled her and the boys down onto the rug.

* * *

Jordan couldn't breathe at the feel of Dylan's hands closing around her waist. Would he notice the extra fifteen pounds of baby fat she still hadn't lost? She landed gently on her back as both the boys continued tickling her.

Laughing, she pulled them against her in defense. "You guys are bad." But she couldn't stop smiling.

Dylan rolled to his side and propped himself up on one elbow. "It's good to see you smile."

Their eyes met for a long second and she wasn't sure what to say. How could he look that gorgeous and sexy and not realize it? Was he like this with Zoe? This time next year, would that other woman be here, sharing these times with Jordan's family?

"Umph!" All the wind rushed out of her as Tristan bounced up and down on her stomach, tickling again.

Dylan peeled him off and hauled him like a sack of potatoes as he pulled the box of Legos they liked from beside the sofa. He snagged Trevor too and sat them on the rug. "I think Mommy's had enough tickling for tonight."

As they tossed Legos out and started snapping them together, Jordan rolled to a sitting position and pushed her hair back. "We need to settle down now and read our book."

"The world isn't going to end if they're late going to bed one night."

"Children need routine."

He cocked an eyebrow. "They also need to learn flexibility."

Okay, so he had a point. It wasn't worth arguing over. "Fine."

Dylan stood and retrieved their coffee while she plopped down on the sofa. "This is still warm, but I can top it off if you want."

She moved to the sofa and took the cup. "It's fine. Thanks."

The cushion gave as he sat beside her and she tried not to be conscious of his leg brushing hers. The situation was way too family-like. Parents sipping coffee while the children played in front of the fire on a stormy evening.

Soon Trevor stretched out and stuck his thumb in his mouth. Sam rested his head on his paws beside him and closed his eyes too.

Dylan leaned around her and flipped off the lamp, leaving only the firelight to illuminate the room. He seemed occupied watching Tristan slowly give up the fight and fall asleep clutching a block in each hand.

Thunder rumbled and rain pelted the window, reminding Jordan of that morning in Florida. One of the rare times the weather had been too stormy to open the Jet Ski rental where they'd worked.

She closed her eyes, lost in the memory...

Their apartment wasn't air-conditioned and the windows were cracked just enough to hear the rain like one of those relaxation CDs. Dylan had turned on the radio and confirmed that there was no sense opening up the business. When she'd come out of the bathroom, he'd been back in bed, no sheet, no clothes and his eyes drooping half asleep.

Heart racing, she leaned her head back against the sofa and willed the image to disappear, but it was more vivid with each raindrop. Dylan had made love to her many times, but she'd never taken the initiative before that day. Not with him. Not with anybody. Her heart had pounded as she straddled his legs, but that lazy grin of his had urged her on, given her the wanton courage to lose her inhibitions. To do things to him that she'd only imagined in the deep dark recesses of her mind. Remembering how she'd used her mouth so intimately brought heat to her face...and lower.

"You remember that rainy morning in Florida?" Dylan's deep voice startled her thoughts.

Realizing that his mind was in the same little apartment, same lumpy bed as hers sent her into a panic. "We need to get the kids to bed."

Before she could stand, he touched her face. "Jordan, don't do this. Don't turn what we had into something to be ashamed of. Whatever happened later, we were awesome together."

Nodding, she focused on the kids, anything except him, but she didn't speak. She couldn't. The rain peppered the windows and the metal roof. And with each drop, she remembered the warmth, the intimacy they'd shared. But things had changed. They were different now. He'd made her vulnerable. It couldn't happen again. "It's past their bedtime."

"They're fine." He grabbed her hand. "Are we going to talk about this?"

"What?" She squelched her panic.

"We're parents of two gorgeous children. We should discuss how we're going to both be a part of their lives."

"Not tonight." She couldn't have a rational conversation with the image of Dylan's naked sweaty body, and steamy sex, and Florida in her mind. Too many conflicting emotions. "You haven't said much about your dad. Did the two of you ever work through your differences? Come to terms?"

That left eye of his narrowed.

Would he allow the change in subject? Did he realize her full panic?

"Well, we never stopped arguing. I wanted to make a success of the ranch and Dad wanted to drink himself into an early grave. He won. He's been gone almost three months and I'm still finding booze stashed in odd places."

She allowed herself to breathe. "But you miss him?"

"Sometimes." He paused. "Mostly I'm just trying to put that crap behind me. Get on with my life. Deep down he wanted me to make something of this place. Turn it back into a profitable business. But no matter how hard I tried, he always reminded me that I could do better."

Which was why Dylan had become a perfectionist. Whatever Dylan McKeon did, he didn't quit until it was the absolute best he could make it. She watched their sons sleeping. Evidently that included baby making. Those boys couldn't be more perfect.

"I know you argued. A lot. But he loved you, Dylan."

He stood and stoked the fire. "Yes, he did."

The intimacy of the room engulfed them in a warm, safe cocoon. Except she felt everything but safe being here with him. "We'd really better get them into bed now. I think Trevor's allergies are turning into a cold."

"I guess Tristan will catch it next?" Dylan sighed as he hauled him up onto his shoulder.

Jordan smiled. "Tristan never gets sick."

"Because he doesn't slow down long enough for germs to catch him."

Jordan carried Trevor to his bed and pulled the blanket over him. She gave him a kiss and watched Dylan kiss the tip of his finger and place it to Tristan's lips. "Love you."

They exchanged places to each tuck in the other twin and Jordan brushed against Dylan. As she straightened from kissing Tristan, she heard Trevor, half asleep, whisper to Dylan. "Wuv you."

Tears sprang to her eyes. *Hold it together*. The first time he'd ever said the word love and he'd said it to his father, not her. Dylan turned and his eyes sparkled with unshed tears too. All the times she'd told the kids she loved them, from before they were born even, yet the first time one of them actually said the word... She had to get out of here. "Goodnight, Dylan."

She crawled into bed, but sleep was illusive. It was stupid to let this upset her. The boys loved her. She should not let this get to her. But it did. Trevor had no idea. He hadn't done it on purpose. He'd just mimicked Dylan's words.

Rolling over, she cradled the pillow. The funny thing was, she was happy that the boys would grow up knowing their father. That they'd know his love. Who'd she been kidding thinking she could give them everything as a single mother? Dylan would be good for them. He was a unique man. She'd learned more about herself with him than from any other person, including her therapist.

When she'd jumped on the back of Dylan's Harley that day after he and her father had argued, she hadn't worried that they had no plan, no money. She'd simply trusted him. And through him, she'd learned to trust her own judgment. She'd worn shorts and tank tops from discount stores and three dollar flip flops. And a burnt orange bikini that she'd felt more comfortable in than clothes her parents had paid ten times the amount for.

Dylan had never pressured her. He'd been patient, let her come to him. She squeezed the pillow. And it had taken her hours, not days to fall under the man's spell.

But she was a mother now. She couldn't afford to indulge her irresponsible side.

Chapter Nine

Jordan felt like she'd just closed her eyes when she awoke to one of the kids crying. She bolted out of bed and was standing in their room before she realized that Dylan was already there. He had on a pair of dull green sleep pants, but no shirt and he was holding Trevor. "He's burning up."

She went for the ear thermometer. "I was afraid of this. He catches everything."

She took the baby from Dylan and sat on the bed. "Maybe a warm washcloth?"

Dylan headed for the bathroom while she held Trevor still and took his temp. Dylan returned with a dripping washcloth.

"It's only 101. Not good, but it could be worse."

"Should we take him to emergency? At least call Doc Howard?"

Jordan bathed Trevor's face, then rocked him against her. "Not yet. Let me see if I can get it down. If he isn't better by morning, we'll see about getting him in somewhere. I'm going to take him into the other room and rock him so he doesn't wake Tristan."

"Here, let me carry him." Dylan waited until she was seated in the rocker, then placed Trevor and his fuzzy blanket in her arms. "Anything I can do?"

Why did the man's shoulders look twice as wide without a shirt? "There's a bottle of infant drops in the diaper bag."

After he handed her the medicine, he hovered. "Want me to build up the fire?"

She shook her head. "No. Just go to bed. When he goes back to sleep, I'll probably just put him in bed with me."

"Okay. Yell if you need anything."

Closing her eyes, she leaned back against the chair, rocking Trevor and trying to put the image of Dylan's bare chest out of her mind. Trevor squirmed and fussed, but finally fell back to sleep. Gently she carried him into her bed and snuggled him under the covers.

Again, she'd no more than dozed off than she heard another cry. Easing out of bed, she found Dylan and Tristan in the kitchen.

Dylan looked a little done-in. "I changed him, but he wouldn't go back to sleep. He feels warm too. I thought maybe a cold drink of water."

Jordan retrieved the thermometer. Dylan sat him on the counter and held him still while she took his temp. "His is barely 100, but he's probably coming down with it too." She tried to give him a dose of medicine, but he clamped his mouth closed and turned away. Sticky pink syrup dribbled off his chin and down the front of his pajamas. "Tristan, hold still."

She held his chin between her fingers and managed to get the next dose into his mouth. He spit part of it out and started wailing.

"He sounds congested," Dylan said.

"Yeah. Here, let me go change his pajamas."

He picked up the boy. "It's just a little stain, don't worry about it."

Her eyes closed. "Okay, then I'll just rock him." That was typically about the only way to settle him down when he was sick. With Tristan, he got sick so seldom that he didn't understand what was wrong.

Dylan cradled him against his shoulder. "I've got this. You take care of Trevor."

* * *

Dylan woke up as the sun came up. Well, it didn't really come up as the rain seemed to have settled into a steady downpour overnight, but at least there was light coming through the blinds. He was stretched out in the recliner, sleeping baby on his chest, and he was sweating.

Jordan had come out to check on Tristan twice and covered them up. This wasn't good. The kid radiated like a tiny heater against his chest. Attempting to adjust his aching muscles, he moved the boy and pulled the blanket down a few inches so they could breathe.

Sam let out a sigh from beside the chair. What was he complaining about? Dylan was the one who'd been woken up every half hour. Yawning, he ran a hand through his hair, pushing it back from his face. He heard noise from the next room. Hopefully Jordan had gotten more sleep.

She came out, Trevor trotting along beside her, lugging his blue blanket and sucking his thumb. "Do you think that doctor you mentioned could get them in today?"

"They open at eight or thereabout. If he can't work them in, there's a minor emergency clinic in Denton."

Neither kid was interested in breakfast so they traded out watching kids so the other one could shower, then got the boys dressed. Doc Howard said to bring them to the office and agreed to work them in. Dylan had the sneaking suspicion he just wanted to get a look at them, make sure they were real. Probably rumors flying all around.

He backed his Dad's king cab pickup into the garage so the kids wouldn't get wet. Luckily when they got to the office, the reception area was empty.

Old Doc Howard's wife came out to greet them. "I heard we had some new folks in the area." She grinned, taking Tristan from Jordan. "Aren't they just the cutest things? Too bad your Papa never got to see them. They'd have had old Mac eating out of their chubby little hands. Come on back."

Jordan followed behind looking a bit bemused by all the attention. Dylan tried to help corral one boy while the doc examined the other. By the time they left, four other people had come in and made a big hurrah over the kids.

The rain had turned into a heavy wet fog while they were in the office. Traffic was light, but those who were out and about moved at a snail's pace. Tires hissed as they rolled down the slick pavement. After a stop by the drug store and another at the grocery store, they finally made it back to the house.

Both kids were sound asleep in their car seats. To Dylan's amazement, they didn't even wake up when they hauled them into bed. They hadn't gotten much sleep the night before and Doc had said the medication he gave them in the office would make them groggy.

As Dylan came out of the kids' room, Jordan was standing in the center of the family room, looking like a walking zombie. Without thinking, he massaged her shoulders. "You're tense."

At first she stiffened, but then gave in and rolled her head back and forth. "They're getting so heavy."

Allowing his fingers to probe and massage, he tried not to think about other times he'd had his hands on her body. Like the massage he'd given her the first evening after she'd ridden on the back of his Harley down the east coast. Only that night she'd been naked, flat of her tummy on a soft bed.

And the massage had led to a hot shower and...

That was after the morning they'd gotten into it with her father and Jordan had stood beside Dylan and faced off against her old man. Possibly the first time ever she'd stood up to him. God she'd looked tough and rebellious when she'd shocked not only her father, but Dylan by tossing a few clothes into a bag and hopping on the Harley behind Dylan. Tied her future to his. Her elation at determining their direction by the flip of a coin. But her initial exuberance had faded after a day of riding. She'd sworn she'd never walk straight again.

He flexed his fingers and ran his hands down her arms, almost pulling her back against him, until he caught himself. Back then she'd trusted him and he'd trusted her. And thinking about the good times only frustrated him because it still made no sense that she'd left. "You hungry?"

"Too exhausted to eat."

Dylan rolled his head. Speaking of food, the animals were probably wondering what happened to him. "You grab a nap and I'll see to the animals."

***

Rain dripped off the brim of his hat as Dylan finished the necessary chores and got back to the house. Might as well haul in some firewood since the chill had already soaked through to the bone. And it had been almost eighty degrees yesterday morning. Crazy Texas weather. Probably be sunshine and short sleeve weather again by the weekend.

As he opened the back door, his eyes tried to adjust to the dim room. All was quiet and not a single light burning. Hauling the wood to the fireplace, he stepped over Sam and found Jordan stretched out asleep on the sofa. Even the dog had opted to stay in warm and dry.

Man, he was whipped. He checked on the boys, and then built up the fire and stretched out in the recliner. With any luck, maybe they would stay asleep long enough for him to grab some shut eye.

Allowing his gaze free reign over Jordan's soft curves, he tried not to think about the past. He couldn't relax with her sleeping five feet away.

Her dark brown hair was all over the place like it always was when she woke up. Just enough curl to give it a mind of its own and enough red highlights to keep life interesting. Sweet face, with eyes that were so big and transparent that he could read her soul when she looked at him, much to her disdain. Her simple white blouse was twisted, exposing the inside of her left breast. A little more full than before. Had she breast-fed the twins? So much he didn't know.

What the heck had happened to change her feelings for him? As hard as he tried to convince himself that their relationship had never been what he'd thought it was, his common sense wasn't biting.

Her eyes fluttered open as she stretched, a tiny grin touching her lips when she noticed the fire. She pointed her nylon covered toes and stretched her arms straight above her head causing her blouse to rise up, leaving at least four inches of skin between it and her black slacks.

His fingers curled.

"Get any rest?"

* * *

Jordan jumped and jerked her head around. Dylan? How long had he been watching her? "I didn't realize I had an audience."

He didn't respond, just cocked a dark eyebrow.

Dim lit room, warm fire, the man that haunted her dreams both night and day. "I should check on the boys."

"They're fine." He eased the recliner to a sitting position and leaned forward, holding her gaze. "Honest answer. What made you leave?"

Feeling intensely vulnerable, she sat up and pulled the hem of her shirt down. "Don't do this. It's all irrelevant now."

"Come on. You owe me the truth. You really didn't know you were pregnant?"

Staring into the depth of those gray-green eyes, she was trapped. She couldn't look away. And she couldn't lie. "I honestly had no idea."

That helped some. "But you were on the pill?"

Jordan shrugged. "Things around here got so chaotic, I forgot a couple times." She realized she should have stopped having sex or at least made sure Dylan used a condom, but living here, the only time she'd felt close to him was late at night, snuggled up in that big bed. That was when she'd had his full attention and she hadn't been willing to risk that or any part of what little she had left of him.

"You forgot?" He refused to look away and she was just as determined not to back down. His left eye narrowed. "So you just fell out of love? Or maybe you never were in love with me?"

"You know I loved you." Her heart threatened to crumble at just the thought of how much she'd loved him, a part of her always would. "But, we're from different worlds. I don't fit in here and you don't fit in New England. We knew that before we even got started."

His eyes were like lasers, burning through her soul. "I didn't know it. And you sure as hell didn't act like you knew it when you spent a year in my arms. You seemed happy, content."

"I was happy, at least until we moved here. You changed, Dylan. You were always busy and when you weren't you were angry."

"Don't throw that up at me. You knew what I was up against with my dad."

She wasn't going to let him off the hook. "The only way the two of you knew to interact was to yell. When I tried to help, you yelled at me."

His eyes widened. "That's called communication. You don't know how to argue."

Didn't know how to argue? "That methodology is counter-productive. It's not healthy. That isn't the way my family communicates." She knew she sounded high handed, but too bad.

"Your family doesn't communicate at all. Your old man dictates and you and your mom obey like good little minions."

"At least we don't yell and scream at one another."

When he stood, she scrambled to her feet. He already had eight inches on her and she wasn't about to allow him to intimidate her by sitting while he towered over her.

He lowered his face to hers. "I yell because I care enough to stay and fight for what I want. I don't run away when things get a little rough. But just for the record, it's when I stop yelling that you might want to worry."

She flinched. "What you and I shared was a lark. A summer fling," she argued, quoting her father.

He leaned closer. "You know better."

As she tried to step around him, he reached out and quickly cupped the back of her neck. His eyes smoldered as smoky and hot as the fire crackling in the rustic stone fireplace. Her gaze slipped downward to his mouth, those lips that could turn her insides to lava with the slightest caress. She gravitated toward him, and then realized she was moving into him without any pressure from the warm fingers massaging her scalp. She could feel his breath on her mouth as her tongue circled her lips, moistening them in preparation for his.

Their lips touched, moved, opening and reawakening the sensations from long ago, or was it yesterday? He was the only man she'd ever let close. The only man who could penetrate her walls, reduce her to an emotional weakling.

He didn't have to crush her against him as he exercised full power with just his kiss. Her eyes fluttered open and she enjoyed how his long dark lashes rested against his cheek as he tilted his head for a better angle. He hadn't shaved since yesterday morning and his stubble grated against her chin, bringing back sexy memories of early mornings waking to his kiss, the touch of his hands on her body.

Lips so soft and so intoxicating, sweet and demanding. This was so right. And so wrong on so many levels.

One hand slipped beneath her shirt and caressed her bare back. Jordan nibbled at his full bottom lip and of their own will, her hands cupped his very fine butt.

"Helllloooo. Anybody home?"

Dylan's eyes opened. "What the hell?"

"Dylllannn." In stark contrast to the gray weather, the voice sing-songed, adding at least one extra syllable to his name.

He rested his forehead against Jordan's and stared into her eyes. "In here, Mom."

Chapter Ten

Daisy Zimmerman breezed into the room like a petite monarch butterfly wearing a pair of flowing burnt yellow pants and a silky fall print blouse. Her long brown hair sported fresh highlights and her face was painted with just enough makeup to accent her cornflower blue eyes.

Jordan backed away from Dylan and switched on the table lamp. She felt like a junior high kid caught making out on the sofa.

Bangle bracelets jingled as Dylan's mom enveloped him in a warm hug, kissed his cheek, and then graced Jordan with the same treatment. "Okay, you two, where are my grandsons?"

"They're sick and napping," Dylan said.

"Oh, I won't wake them," Daisy said, already in route to the spare room. Dylan followed, but Jordan hung back, taking a moment to regain her composure after that all-consuming kiss.

Pressing both hands against her belly, she attempted to squelch the quivering. She grimaced at her reflection in the narrow mirror inside the grandfather clock. What little makeup she'd applied this morning was mostly gone and what was left was smeared in dark circles beneath her sleep-deprived eyes. Swiping at it with her thumbs only made it worse. But Daisy was so engrossed in the new adventure of having grandsons that she wouldn't notice.

Slowly Jordan eased her way to the door where Dylan was introducing his mother to the boys in muffled whispers. Dylan shoved the sleeves up on his navy blue sweater and Jordan tried not to stare at his arms. That was the same sweater he'd had on the first night they'd...the first night. That stupid kiss had her emotions all out of sorts.

He reached over and adjusted Trevor's blanket and the boy's eyes popped open. They'd been asleep over two hours, so it was probably best that they woke up anyway. He took one look at Daisy and reached his arms for Dylan. "Papa."

Dylan lifted him up grinning from ear to ear. He looked at Jordan. "Did you hear that? He said Papa."

She nodded and smiled, not sure whether the feeling bubbling up from deep in her heart was happiness or fear. There was a strange magnetism about Dylan that drew people, and animals, to him. Earned him unconditional trust.

The expression on Daisy's face was pure bliss. "I remember the first time you said Papa. You had Mac eating out of your hand from that moment forward. You were his boy."

Dylan cradled his son's head against his shoulder and turned to Daisy. "Trevor, this is your grandmother."

Daisy beamed as she patted his back. "How about you call me Daisy? Grandmother is way too big of a word for such a teeny little fellow. Can you say Daisy?"

Trevor screwed up his mouth, head still buried in Dylan's shoulder. "Daee."

"Delightful. I love it. Oh, it's perfect."

Daisy's exuberance was too excited and chaotic for Tristan to sleep through. He sat up, rubbing his eyes.

Daisy squatted down beside his bed. "Hi there."

Jordan wanted to go to him, make sure he felt secure, but he actually didn't look spooked. Instead he got the most adorable, confused expression on his face. A look very much like the one she'd seen on his father's face more than once recently when dealing with the twins. His gaze darted from Daisy, to Jordan, to Dylan, then back to Daisy.

Daisy grinned. "Oh my. They're just the most amazing little guys in the world. Grandmother Daisy brought gifts." She waved her hands in the air, bangle bracelets jingling. "Lots and lots of gifts."

Tristan's confusion melted into smiles as he reached for the shiny metal that was making such wonderful noises. Daisy handed him a solid silver bracelet and glanced over her shoulder at Dylan. "Would you mind getting my bags? The keys are in the car."

Of course they were. This was free spirited Daisy who would never bother to lock the car. Judging by when Jordan had met her after Mac's accident, she wouldn't be surprised if the car was still running. No telling what she'd brought. Jordan could only hope whatever it was wasn't alive.

Dylan placed Trevor on the floor and headed for the door. As he passed Jordan, their arms brushed and he winked. "And you thought life was crazy before. Now we have three children to corral."

Crazy progressed to crazier with the arrival of Daisy Zimmerman's luggage. She took a boy by each hand and followed Dylan into the master bedroom that she'd shared with Mac when she was in town. Two enormous red cases. The larger of the two reminded Jordan of a clown car. There was no bottom in the thing. There couldn't be or she'd have never gotten that many toys in it. An activity box, books, videos, two big yellow dump trucks to push and a nylon tube that sprang open as soon as she put it on the floor. The room filled with jingles, chimes, and giggles as the boys bounced around. Just as they got interested in one thing, she pulled something else out.

Trevor dropped down on all fours and took off through the nylon tube. A set of little cars clattered and honked as Daisy pushed them across the wood floor.

Sam stood to the side, studying the suitcase until Daisy tossed him a bright colored doggy rope to chew on.

"Aren't these the cutest things!" Daisy handed each boy different light up toys. One was a turtle and the other a fish. "I had no idea what the kids were into so I bought a little of everything. I had to ship a couple big boxes."

"Really? I figured you just chartered your own plane shaped like a sleigh with a red light on the nose," Dylan quipped.

The big yellow dump truck clattered as Tristan pushed it across the floor at about a thousand miles per hour. Trevor was still enthralled with the bright red tube.

Jordan put her hands over her ears.

"Was that barbeque in the front seat for dinner? We missed lunch," Dylan asked.

Daisy grinned as she zipped the other suitcase open. "Oh, yeah. I stopped at that place you like in Denton on my way from the airport. Hope you have cold beer."

"There's no alcohol in this house. Coffee?" Without waiting on her answer, he turned and headed toward the kitchen.

Jordan stared after him. He'd never been one to drink much, but they'd enjoyed an occasional beer or margarita. Of course, Mac had been an alcoholic.

"Look at these wonderful little outfits. Dylan didn't know whether they wore eighteen or twenty-four month so I bought some of each. I just fell in love with this one." Daisy tossed two little outfits on the bed. Black corduroy pants and one gray and one black stripe sweater. "They'll look like teenagers without the smarty attitude."

Dylan had always claimed that money was no object for Daisy. She was a makeup artist in Hollywood and seemed to always be in demand. Her father had been in the movie business, but Jordan couldn't recall exactly what he did. Lighting or sound maybe.

One of Daisy's favorite stories was about the time her father hauled her with him to Texas where he was working on a movie because her mother thought she was out of control. Mac had been an extra in a rodeo scene and Daisy had taken one look at those wide shoulders and been in his bed that very afternoon.

Trevor squealed as Tristan crawled after him through the tube.

Jordan blinked at the growing mountain of little boy outfits on the bed. They'd outgrow these before they had a chance to wear half of them. Finally Daisy reached the end of the kids' clothes and hung some of her own outfits in the closet. "I had such fun shopping."

One second Daisy was hanging clothes in the closet and the next down on all fours crawling through the tube chasing Tristan. "Better hurry. Daisy's gonna get you."

"I'll go help Dylan heat up dinner. Just sing out if you need me."

She found Dylan making coffee. "Here, I'll set the table."

"Thanks."

She couldn't get the alcohol comment out of her mind. "I guess things got pretty rough toward the end with your dad."

"Yep."

"But you did make peace?"

Dylan pushed the button on the coffee maker and turned to her. He put his hands on the bar and leaned back against them. "For the most part."

"But you don't allow alcohol in the house?" She watched his face harden. "I don't understand. You aren't an alcoholic. You're a stronger man than he was."

"Damn straight. No woman is going to do to me what my mother did to him. Not you. Not anybody." He yanked his denim jacket off the hook by the back door.

"Dylan."

"I lost my appetite!"

Jordan flinched as the door slammed shut behind him. What the heck? The emotional outburst reminded her of when she'd lived here two years ago. She pressed her hand to her stomach. How was she supposed to figure out what was going to trigger his temper?

* * *

Dylan was still shaking when he reached the barn. The rain pelting his skin hadn't even begun to cool him down. He hung his jacket on the corner of Cinder's stall and headed away from the horses, to the back of the barn and his punching bag.

Maybe he'd over-reacted.

Like hell he did.

When Jordan had left him, he'd damn near become his father, but it wouldn't happen again. No woman was going to do that to him. Not even if he did love her. And at the moment, his feelings were so tangled up with Jordan and the kids, he wasn't sure what he felt. His father had idolized his mother and look where that had gotten him.

Every time his mother came for a visit she stayed just long enough to get his dad all worked up and hopeful that this time she'd stay, and every single time she left. And with each visit, his father had sunk just a little further into the bottle. Yet he'd always welcomed her back.

Dylan tossed his shirt aside, wrapped his hands in tape and took a swing at the free hanging punching bag. It felt good to get into the rhythm. Right-left-right. The speed ball vibrated as he continued to pound it. Rain peppered against the tin roof and the barn smelled musty.

He loved his parents. But their relationship had been like a volatile chemistry experiment gone bad. The passion erupted and consumed them. One minute they'd be in each other's faces arguing over some insane nothing and the next they'd stumble into the bedroom for make-up marathons that lasted into the next day, or week.

No doubt they'd loved each other, but not enough. Not enough for Daisy to commit and stay with her man like normal couples. Dylan slammed his fist into the bag.

Until he found someone who wanted to share his life, forever after, good and bad, ink on a marriage license and rings on their fingers, he wasn't settling. Other couples had that, so what was wrong with the McKeon men that women felt no such inclination?

He paused. Well, okay, maybe he and Jordan had drifted apart toward the end, but he'd actually been foolish enough to believe that they were in it for the long haul.

Yeah, now that was foolish.

Jordan had left once. She'd do it again.

He just had to try to ignore her when he could and not fight with her the rest of the time. Just concentrate on the boys. They were what mattered.

He could be a good father without a wife.

And as much as it always irritated him when Jordan put on her counselor hat and tried to fix him, she was right about one thing. He was stronger than his father.

God, he shouldn't have kissed her.

* * *

Dylan rolled over on his back and pulled the blanket up. He'd stayed in the barn long enough for Jordan to be in bed before coming inside. He listened to the quiet house. Maybe with the aid of the medicine the doctor had prescribed, the boys would sleep through the night. He could use some time to get his head together and figure out how he was going to get through the next week with Jordan in this house and not succumb to his attraction to her.

It felt like he'd just closed his eyes when he heard one of the twins coughing. Stumbling out of bed, he tried to focus. Trevor was asleep, but Tristan was sitting up in bed. Without turning on a light, he reached his arms down and Tristan came into them.

"Hey buddy, let's go find your medicine."

The kid felt hot against Dylan's chest. He flipped on the light over the kitchen sink and read the pad where Jordan was tracking when she gave each boy his meds. He sat Tristan on the counter and reached for the bottle. "Yeah, you're overdue."

Tristan clamped his mouth shut and shook his head back and forth even before Dylan could measure the dosage. "Tell you what. Take your medicine like a big boy and Papa will give you a cookie."

Tristan narrowed one eye as if considering whether he'd actually get a cookie. Or maybe whether it was even worth it. "Come on. It's grape."

At the first slight opening of Tristan's mouth, Dylan squirted the medicine in. Only a little purple sticky gunk trickled out one corner of his mouth. He held a cup for him to take a sip of water then gave him the cookie he'd promised. The kid's cheeks looked rosy and hot. He wiped down Tristan's face, unzipped his sleeper and wiped his chest.

Dylan needed sleep and the kid looked wide-eyed. "Let's get dry britches, and then you can sleep with Papa."

* * *

Jordan woke up to the sun coming through the blinds and squinted at the clock. Six AM. And she hadn't woken up to give the boys their medication. She bolted out of bed. The house was quiet, but the boys weren't in their beds. Frantically she raced into Dylan's room and slid to a stop at the foot of his king-sized bed.

He was asleep on the edge, flat of his back with Trevor snuggled against his side. Trevor had been wearing blue pajamas to match Tristan when she'd put the boys down for the night. The fact that he now had on green ones was a pretty good indication that Dylan had contended with more than a messy diaper.

Tristan was in the center of the bed, caged on the far side by pillows to keep him from falling off the tall bed. His face didn't looked flushed like it had when she'd put him down last night.

The boys had woken up, Dylan had taken care of them, and she'd never heard a peep.

In twenty months, it had always been she who heard them, who got up and took care of whatever the problem was.

She sucked in a breath at the sight of Dylan, his son snuggled securely in the crook of his arm. His square jaw was relaxed. Those thick dark lashes rested gently against his cheek bones. The sheet only came up to his waist and the room was a little chilly, but one foot stuck out from beneath the bottom of the sheet. She grinned. He'd always insisted that he couldn't breathe with both feet under the covers.

It would be so simple to fall back under his spell, but she didn't belong here anymore. It didn't matter that she'd spent some of the most incredible nights of her life in this bed. This was Dylan's room. It was no longer hers. She touched the tip of her tongue to her top lip, remembering the kiss from the day before. Why had he suddenly gotten so angry?

She hadn't belonged here before, and he sure didn't want her here now. He'd already told her she could leave anytime. This visit was all about the boys.

Her gaze wandered back up and she froze, finding his eyes focused on her.

"Did you make coffee?" he asked.

"I-I will," she stammered, trying to act normal. He knew she'd been studying him. "Thanks for taking care of the boys. I really needed the sleep."

He eased Trevor closer to Tristan and sat up. She breathed a sigh of relief finding that he had on navy plaid sleep pants. When they'd been together, he'd often slept in the buff. So had she.

As he stood, she knew that he knew exactly where her mind had gone. Much to her annoyance, the guy had always been able to read her thoughts. He'd said her eyes were like a telescope into her mind.

He rolled his head back and forth and then looked at her. Reaching out, he rested a hand against her cheek. "Whatever we did wrong before, we did one thing right with the twins. Gotta wonder what we'll do to screw them up."

He'd once told her that his parents should have been required to pass a test and get a license to be parents. "Just because our parents weren't great role models, doesn't mean that we can't be good parents. We can learn from their mistakes."

He cocked his head. "Well there are plenty of mistakes to learn from."

She shrugged. "We'll figure it out."

"Coffee." He looked her straight in the eye. "I need coffee."

"Right, coffee." She scurried toward the kitchen, eager to escape from the intimacy of Dylan's bedroom. But it worried her that he still seemed caught up in negativity with his father. She put the coffee pot on and found a can of cinnamon rolls in the fridge. She hadn't eaten much after his little temper tantrum the night before.

By the time Dylan appeared, she had the rolls in the oven and two cups on the counter. He still had on the sleep pants, but he'd combed his hair and put on a gray tee shirt. He eased the pot out of the coffee machine before it even stopped dripping and filled the two cups. Evidently waiting another couple minutes wasn't an option today.

He handed her one of the cups. "I wrote down what time I gave them medicine. Tristan was sweating, but he cooled down after the meds."

Nodding, she took the cup. "He doesn't get sick as often as Trevor, but when he does it hits him harder. Did you get any sleep?"

"Some. Tristan tosses and kicks, but Trevor is as cuddly as a puppy."

"Yep." She glanced at the empty glass fronted cabinet over the sink that had once contained liquor. Her common sense said she shouldn't pry. His problems were no longer hers and were none of her business. But her mouth wasn't listening. "So your father really got worse toward the end?"

"His liver was shot, but he never quit drinking. I wish I had the money for all the booze I poured down the drain, but he just bought more. Finally one night when he finished one bottle and dug another out from behind a book in the case, I lost it. At first I yanked it away from him, like I'd done more than once. Then I just gave up. Took the stopper out and handed it back. Told him that if he wanted to kill himself, have at it."

"And?" She wasn't sure if he'd continue. She couldn't make Dylan talk if he didn't want to. If he wanted her to know more, he'd tell her.

"And he drank it." Dylan left his untouched coffee on the bar and walked to the window.

Jordan followed and put her hand on his back. "There was nothing you could have done if he wasn't willing to change."

He nodded.

"You've buried your father, Dylan. Can you finally move past that? Get on with your life."

"I'm trying."

Except then he'd discovered she hadn't told him about the twins, and now he had to deal with that. But that she decided, was a conversation for another time.

She dropped her hand. After the kiss yesterday, touching him felt way too comfortable and not comfortable at all. Too many conflicting emotions. She couldn't think rationally when she let her emotions surface.

"When I was mucking the stalls, Rusty came by. He has no doubt you'll be able to help the horse. He says you possess some sort of magic with animals."

"Yeah? Well horses are easier to understand than people. They may kick your brains out on occasion, but you know where you stand with them. Or sit, when they land you on your ass. But basically you just wait, let them get used to you, and they'll come to you on their own."

Hmm, similar to the way he'd handled the boys. He hadn't rushed them or pushed them, just made himself available and let them get accustomed to him. And they had come to him. She blinked. Come to think of it, that same low-key strategy had worked pretty well on her.

Could she remain immune to his charms?

Chapter Eleven

The twins awoke free of fever and back to their bouncy, non-stop selves. Dylan helped Jordan feed them, then hugged them and took off to the barn before his mom woke up. Jordan had to smile. She wasn't sure what his hurry was since Daisy seldom showed her face before noon.

The boys were watching one of their new videos, surrounded by toys when Daisy made her appearance. Jordan glanced at the clock, barely nine o'clock. Daisy breezed out of the bedroom, a bright flowing caftan whishing around her ankles, plopped down in the center of the rug with the boys and started pushing buttons. The volume in the room quadrupled. When the characters on the video started singing the ABC song, Daisy joined in, singing at the top of her lungs as if it was her favorite song of all time.

Trevor sat back and cocked his head unsure what to make of this strange person. Tristan started bouncing and singing. Daisy stood and took them both by the hand, dancing in a circle as she continued to sing.

Jordan shook her head. Life was never dull with Daisy in the house. No wonder she brought Mac to life. How could anyone ignore her exuberance? Yet, she could understand how it wore Dylan down after a while.

When Daisy finally danced her way into the kitchen, Jordan had finished cleaning up the breakfast dishes. "I could scramble you some eggs."

"No, no." Poo-pooing her away with one hand, Daisy noted the coffee pot and pulled out three mugs. She filled them all, splashed cream into two of them then held up the carton. "Do you take cream?"

"No."

Daisy replaced the coffee carafe and handed Jordan one of the mugs with cream and the one that was black. "Why don't you run down to the stable and take Dylan a fresh cup. I'll just stay here and get to know my grandsons."

Unsure how to respond graciously without making the requested trek to the stable, Jordan slipped on Dylan's leather jacket that was hanging by the back door. Leaving the boys at the mercy of Daisy, Jordan retrieved the two mugs and made her way to the stables.

As she approached, Jordan studied Dylan forking fresh hay into the stalls. She stopped short and let her eyes drink their fill. He still had that body. Not a muscle builder, but muscles built from hard work. As he turned and caught her staring at him, she felt her face heat. Just like the day she'd first met him in Colorado when he'd turned from playing pool and caught her checking him out. Her heart had threatened to jump out of her chest as Dylan had let his gaze leisurely roam down her body, then back to her face. The act had felt as sensual as any actual caress.

Then he'd handed off the pool cue and changed the course of Jordan's life with a single word, "Dance?"

Dylan propped the pitchfork against the fence, removed his hat and shoved his hair off his face before replacing the hat. He nodded toward the two mugs she was holding. "Is one of those for me?"

She blinked away her memories and handed him the mug, praying she wasn't actually blushing. "When did you start drinking cream in your coffee?"

He leaned on the corral with a sideways grin and took the mug. "I don't. Mom's wires are crossed. Dad liked cream."

"So tell her." Jordan took a sip of her black coffee and tried to ignore the trickle of sweat running down the center of his chest.

"I have, repeatedly." He wrapped his hand around the mug. "Told you she's quirky."

"Well, the kids think she's a toy solely for their entertainment." The rescued horse stalked to the other side of the round pen and sized Jordan up. So sad that someone would mistreat an animal to the extent it didn't trust. But then again, some people treated other people even worse. "What's the purpose of a round pen?"

"There's no corner for the horse to hide in."

"Never thought about that." She paused, glancing at the small herd of cows in the north pasture. "I thought you didn't like cows."

He cocked an eyebrow. "Yeah, well they bring in money."

"Ahhh." She nodded. "Guess I'd better go rescue the boys. Left them at the mercy of your mom."

"Good plan. She'll have them swinging on the chandelier right along beside her."

"You don't have a chandelier," Jordan quipped, taking his empty mug and heading back to the house.

Some upbeat pop tune greeted her before she got within fifty feet of the back patio. As she opened the door, she came to a stop, transfixed by the spectacle. The boys and Daisy were all bouncing around the great room. When the song ended, Daisy fell down to the rug, laughing. The boys sat down then lay back beside her, playing along with the antics of their new Daisy toy.

The sound of a passing vehicle distracted Jordan and she walked over to the window. Either Rusty's or Zoe's, and she'd take bets this one was candy apple red. Tilting the blinds, she grimaced. Of course it was Zoe. The woman had to check on the horse, after all. Jordan scolded herself for being sarcastic, but the horse would be fine for one day without the redhead.

"So are you going to let her steal your man right from beneath your nose?"

Jordan flinched at Daisy's accusation. "He's not my man anymore."

Daisy leaned in beside Jordan and watched Dylan saunter up to Zoe's pickup and open her door. "Well, that girl's been catting around here for going on a year now. I gotta think it's not entirely about the horses."

Jordan turned from the window and pushed her hair back. "Whatever is between them has nothing to do with me."

Continuing to look unashamedly out the window, Daisy shrugged. "Hmm."

She did not have to listen to Daisy's unsolicited opinion. Jordan tromped into the great room and turned the stereo volume down. She scooped Trevor up. "You need a dry diaper, baby?"

Still, music filled the house the remainder of the day. Never a quiet moment. But at least the woman's taste was eclectic. Soft jazz, contemporary, country. Daisy danced or floated through the day, humming or singing to whatever tune was playing, giving each her full out best effort.

"I never cook at home, but I become so domestic in this house. Mac had this kitchen custom designed for me. Don't you love the new countertops?" Daisy caressed a hand over the granite.

Jordan nodded. "They're beautiful."

"The little munchkins are down for a nap. Just tuckered right out they did. And right in the middle of Lego Land."

"They're still recovering from their colds," Jordan explained, although at twenty months, they took naps whether they'd been playing with a wild woman all morning or not.

"I've got dinner tonight." Daisy said, shooing Jordan out of the kitchen. "You do like beef stroganoff, no?"

"Sure. If you don't mind, I'm going to try to get a little work done while the kids are down." And while Dylan was out of the house.

* * *

By the time Dylan saw to the horses and finished the chores, he was beat and hoping for a little downtime. But music vibrated the walls. Daisy had arrived, no denying that. After dinner, they all retired to the family room, but Daisy still hadn't slowed down. As the stereo switched to an upbeat tune, she grabbed the boys by the hand. "Dylan, I can't believe you haven't taught your sons to dance. You should be ashamed."

He dropped into the leather recliner and grinned at her. "You seem to have the situation under control."

Jordan curled up on the sofa with her laptop and seemed to tune the commotion out. She certainly hadn't been raised in the kind of chaos his mother generated. He hadn't been in her parents' house that many times, but he didn't remember ever hearing music of any kind.

Daisy only let him sit out the one song before grabbing his hand and tugging him to his feet. "You remember this one. It was one of Mac's favorite tunes."

All he wanted to do was rest his aching muscles, but he took his mom into his arms and danced her around the room to an old George Strait song. "Good memories, huh?"

Sniffing, she leaned her head back and looked him in the eyes.

He was too tired to deal with this. "You okay?"

"Of course." In typical Daisy fashion, she tossed her hair back and flashed a beaming smile. "We're leaving poor Jordan out. You dance with her and I'll dance with these two good lookin' gentlemen."

Dancing. Jordan. Not the best plan.

He dropped his arms from his mom's shoulders. "It's the kids' bath time."

* * *

By the time the boys had drenched his bathroom and played in the tub until the water was cold, Dylan had calmed down. Having Jordan in the same house was hard enough without his mom suggesting dancing. There was no future for them, so why even go down that road.

He dried each boy and wrapped them in big fluffy towels, then herded them into their room. He managed to get diapers on both of them, but Tristan took off while he sacked Trevor into an ugly zoo animal print sleeper. Leaving him to play, he snatched a solid blue sleeper out of the drawer and took off after Tristan.

"Sure you don't need any help?" Jordan looked up from her laptop as he snagged the boy.

"Nah, I've got it." Tristan giggled as Dylan tossed him upside down over his shoulder, then dumped him unceremoniously onto the bed. "Thought you could get away from me, did you?"

Sitting down on the bed, he tried to stuff four wiggling appendages into the one piece sleeper. He managed to get three in and start on the last, but Tristan had managed to pull one arm out. "Could you be still?"

"Wait, he has one like Trevor's." Just as he finally got all the parts in the right arms or legs, Jordan decided to get involved?

If she thought he was going to pull this one off now that he finally got the kid into it, she was nuts. "So he can sleep in it tomorrow night."

"But they like to be dressed alike."

Dylan plopped Tristan on the floor and he joined his brother beside the Lego bin. "Hmm, they don't really seem to notice."

She scowled, but didn't offer any more ridiculous arguments. Instead she bent down and kissed each boy. "I love you. Mommy is going to take a shower. You two be good and go to sleep for Papa." She glanced at Dylan. "Don't forget their meds."

His mother had outdone herself wearing the boys out today. Dylan gave them their medication and by the end of the first book, both were out cold. He placed Trevor in his bed and tucked him in then did the same for Tristan, but they neither one even batted an eyelid.

As he turned out the light and left the room, his mother met him. She sat on the sofa and indicated he should sit too. Jordan was nowhere in sight and the door to her room was shut. All he wanted was a shower and a soft bed, but he complied with Daisy's wish. What was another half an hour?

"You've been avoiding me."

Dylan kicked back in the recliner. "I've been busy, Mom. Not avoiding you."

She got that concerned mother look on her face that always indicated that she was going to claim that she wasn't going to pry, but then pry anyway. "I realize you're a grown man and this whole relationship between you and Jordan is none of my business."

"Correct on both counts." Maybe she'd drop the subject.

She finger combed her long hair back and stared him in the eye. "But you know and I know that she's the one."

He was so not up to this tonight. "Right. She's the one who left. She's the one who purposely kept my sons a secret."

"So talk to her. You're in love with her, Dylan. Your father knew it. He left half the ranch to her so you'd have to deal with her. But more importantly, you know it. I can see it every time you two look at one another."

Enough of this crap. Like he hadn't realized why his father had left Jordan half the ranch. "Mom, take this for what it's worth. Your perception of love isn't exactly the norm. You loved Dad for what, thirty five years and never married him. Or even lived with him full time. Explain to me what makes you the expert."

Undaunted, Daisy stared him down. "I dare you to find any other couple who loved one another with anything close to the depth that Mac and I did. And we knew the minute you brought Jordan home, that she was the one for you. She's your soul mate like I was Mac's and he was mine."

"Soul mate? Soul mates stay together through good and bad." With a quick release of the lever, Dylan let the recliner down. He was already headed toward his room before his feet landed on the floor. "I respect that your relationship worked for you and Dad. No commitment, a marriage license is just a piece of paper, if you love someone set them free and all that crap. But I'm not willing to settle. Ain't gonna happen."

* * *

Jordan couldn't read Daisy's mood the next day. Again she played with the boys and the house was filled with music. But something was different. The music leaned toward old country and the expression on the older woman's face was...nostalgic. Jordan watched as she picked up a picture off the shelf, caressed it, then replaced it, putting a great deal of effort in angling it just so.

Later, Jordan came out of the study from working on a case and found Trevor asleep on the rug in front of the fireplace and Daisy rocking Tristan. She ran a hand down his cheek then looked up at Jordan. "Genes. Tristan looks identical to Dylan's baby pictures. With the exception of maybe the style of clothing, I bet you couldn't tell one from the other. And Dylan looks so much like Mac did at thirty." Tears swamped her tone, not just her eyes. "He would have loved these boys so much and he'll never know them."

"I'm sorry about that." One more person she'd kept them from.

"Oh no, I'm not blaming you. I would just love to see him with them. He had so much love. I miss that man every second of every day. A part of me died with Mac McKeon."

Jordan squatted down beside the chair and wrapped an arm around Daisy. She tried to convince herself that she didn't understand what Daisy was feeling, her unconditional love for Mac. But she got it. Oh man, did she get it. But if Dylan had ever felt that toward Jordan, she'd destroyed it by leaving him. "Mac was a special man. He was so welcoming when Dylan brought me here." At least when he was sober. With the exception of the time Daisy came to help out, mostly the man drank and slept.

"The house just isn't the same. It was made for love. And these boys...." Daisy's voice faded away.

Jordan straightened, but Daisy grabbed her hand. "I don't know what's going on with you and Dylan, but you need to talk. You need to work things out, decide what's best for these precious little people."

"I know." Jordan shrugged, not wanting to worry Daisy. "We'll get to it."

"You and Dylan haven't had a minute without the kids. You can't get down to business with them under foot. I'm keeping them tonight and you two go out to dinner. Relax. The kids will be fine with me."

Jordan shook her head. Being alone for an entire evening without the kids as a buffer was dangerous. She didn't want to be any more vulnerable to Dylan than she already was. "I don't think..."

"You two need to make a decision about these babies. I'm not taking no for an answer."

* * *

Jordan dressed in jeans, her favorite brown cashmere sweater, and as an afterthought squeezed her feet into her high heeled boots. She told herself that she just needed to feel like more than a mom tonight. It had been a long time since she'd thought of herself as a woman. Well, not exactly true. But over the past couple years, embracing her womanly side had fallen somewhere down the priority list below mother, student, intern and therapist.

When the Harley revved up, she almost backed out. Dylan had agreed for the two of them to go out to dinner, but she'd figured the pickup. Maybe Daisy's little rented sedan. But no, Dylan had to choose the Harley. Was he baiting her?

She looked through the front window and studied Dylan straddling the motorcycle. Dark sunglasses. Jeans, boots, and his leather jacket. She'd take bets that one of his black tee-shirts was beneath that jacket. Like the Marlborough Man, sans the horse, and the cigarette, and the cowboy hat. Okay, so maybe the scale tipped a little more on the Harley Davidson side than Marlborough Man, but there was a kinship to each.

She wanted to question his choice of transportation, but decided not to give him the satisfaction of admitting it made her uncomfortable. Not uncomfortable for her safety, she'd never been afraid riding with Dylan. She'd been the length of the east coast and half way across the country behind him on that thing. More uncomfortable with her body being in such close proximity to his body.

With a resigned sigh, she snatched a light jacket from the closet just as there was a knock on the front door.

She opened the door and Dylan grinned. "You ready?"

She zipped her jacket and nodded.

He looked his fill, slowly making his way from her face down to her jacket, pausing at her breasts, then sliding down her legs, then back to her eyes. Her body burned.

"You sure you'll be warm enough? Supposed to get down around fifty tonight."

"I'm fine." She hated the telltale, breathless sound to her voice. She tossed her hair back and kissed each boy, then reminded Daisy that her cell number was on the bar along with the kids' doctor back home, just in case.

Daisy hardly looked up from the movie she and the boys were engrossed in. "Yes ma'am. They're all on the pad beside the phone. Got it. We're good."

Jordan took Dylan's arm and stepped out on the porch, feeling the sunshine kiss her face. "Beautiful afternoon."

"That it is." He placed a black helmet on her head. She closed her eyes and tried not to react as his fingers grazed the sensitive skin at her throat as he buckled the strap.

"Ready?"

Staring into the gray-green depths, it seemed as if he was asking about more than just a motorcycle ride. Memories swamped her soul, squeezing the breath from her lungs. Of riding behind him, her arms wrapped tight around his waist, her cheek pressed against his hot back, and the masculine scent of Dylan enveloping her as they roared down the highway. The exhilarating feeling of freedom and wild possibilities.

A long time ago, Jordan.

As she climbed on behind him, he buckled his helmet and gave the motorcycle some gas. The vibration between her legs buzzed through her body as her legs bracketed Dylan. The intimacy of the position sent her heart racing faster than the monster engine. Hesitating, she waited until the last minute to wrap her arms around his stomach.

They took it easy down the gravel road, across the bridge over the creek until the road met the main highway. A couple egrets stood in the edge of the stock tank, glowing white against the murky water.

As Dylan turned onto the two-lane blacktop, he accelerated and Jordan tightened her grasp.

Streaks of pink and orange painted the sky as the sun began to set, silhouetting a huge barn as they sped past. Horses and cows grazed in fields still green enough in November to remind Jordan that this was Texas, not Connecticut. Dylan slowed as he came up behind a rancher creeping along in front of them on some huge machine. Dylan didn't try to speed around him, didn't even seem the least bit impatient. She'd forgotten that about him. He took things as they came, never rushing through life.

After crossing a bridge, the rancher moved over on the shoulder and motioned them around with his bright green cap. He and Dylan exchanged waves as they passed. She wondered whether they knew each other or were just being polite.

Invigorated by the crisp, clean air and the smell of fresh cut hay, Jordan began to relax. The constant responsibility of the kids and the job began to melt away. As quirky as Dylan's hippy-dippy mother was, she did trust her with the boys.

They crossed a long bridge over some lake and Dylan turned into the parking lot of a marina. Rows of sailboats, motorboats and fishing boats filled slips.

He pulled into a parking space and killed the engine. Jordan threw her leg over and started removing her helmet as Dylan did the same. She glanced at the bait and tackle shop. "Do I have to fish for my dinner?"

He grinned. "You might."

Placing his hand on the small of her back, he escorted her down a boardwalk, across a small bridge and into a little restaurant with a flashing sign that touted the original name, 'The Fish Shack'.

They opted for a corner booth beside the window with an open view of the lake. As dusk fell, fishermen chugged into the marina, the lights from their boats reflecting off the dark water. Jordan ordered dinner and a glass of wine, but paused when Dylan ordered black coffee. "You, umm. Do you mind if I have a glass of wine?"

He shook his head. "Not at all."

"I could have coffee."

"Have the wine. You could use a little relaxation." Dylan waved the waiter away.

Dylan never had been much of a drinker, but he used to have a beer or glass of wine with her. No alcohol in the house? Coffee with a nice dinner? An alcoholic father? "You don't drink at all anymore, do you?"

"No."

"Since your father's death?"

"Since a couple years ago." He finger combed his hair back from his face. "Did you hear Tristan this afternoon? He said Papa as plain as day when I came in. Not Pop, but Papa."

Okay? Subject changed.

She studied Dylan's beaming face and couldn't keep from returning the grin. "I heard. It seems they pick up at least a couple new words every day now."

Dylan sat back as the waiter served their drinks. How many meals had they shared? A year's worth. He took a drink and stared out as a pleasure barge eased into the marina. They both knew they were here to discuss the kids, but he didn't seem to have any more of an idea how to approach that subject without triggering a fight than she did.

Dinner progressed quietly, not even much small talk, but afterwards, Dylan ordered her another glass of wine and himself more coffee. She just watched him, waited to see what he was going to say.

"I'm not going to ask why you left me. I'm not even going to push for why you didn't contact me when you found out you were pregnant or at least when the kids were born." He took a drink of coffee and leveled that intense Dylan gray-green stare on her. "I don't want to argue anymore. At this point, it's about what's best for the twins."

"Agree." She hadn't wanted the wine, but gulped down a third of it before continuing. "It will be easier as they get older, but for the next few years, I can't imagine letting them come here without me. Nothing against you or your ability to take care of them, I just can't let them be that far away from me."

"Okay. Let's go with that for a minute. What if we designated a couple times a year that you and the boys come here? Maybe when I get the ranch back into a profitable venture, I can fly to Hartford one of those times. But right now, I'm struggling and time off just isn't feasible."

Direct, honest, to the point. "I figured." She'd seen him working at the computer in the study late the other night and heard a couple conversations. Not creditors, but selling hay and arranging to work with somebody's son and the horse they'd just bought. He'd rented out five acres of pasture to a guy with a couple horses. He was playing every angle to make the ranch pay. "I realize cash is scarce right now and you can't afford child support. Which is why the smart thing for me to do to insure the boys future is to keep my half the ranch."

This way, even if Dylan married someone else and had other children, Jordan could be guaranteed that Tristan and Trevor would get at least half his assets.

"I can't believe you're bargaining with my ranch and I'm letting you get away with it." He said, but he grinned. "Still, the kids are the first priority." He narrowed his eyes. "But I do want the title back at some point." He let out a breath. "I'll figure out how to pay something. Won't be much at first, but they are as much my responsibility as yours. I'll have a will drawn up and leave everything to the kids. Make you the executor. Don't have a problem with that."

"Okay. I'll do the same. Not that I have much right now."

A couple across the restaurant waved and Dylan returned the gesture. "The Griffins. Their son, Tom, and I were buddies. I'm sure they'll enjoy validating the rumor that you're back."

"I'm not back, Dylan. Not in that way." She tilted her head and looked at him. The heat in his eyes burned through her. She stared into that face and swore she could hear the surf pounding. They were back at that little seafood restaurant in Florida with only four tables on the dock. The one with no air conditioning and the best gulf shrimp she'd ever tasted.

"You remember Cap'n Jacks?" he asked.

"That's the name. I was just thinking about that place. I distinctly remember one night there when my calm and logic saved you from a fist fight."

Dylan picked up his coffee. "Yeah, well, that guy was out of line."

"He was drunk," Jordan clarified.

Dylan cocked his head and grinned. "You never did tell me what psycho-babble you fed him that made him stop coming on to you."

"Oh, it was textbook." She nibbled on a French fry. "I told him that my boyfriend had just gotten out of prison. Something about attempted murder."

At the sound of Dylan's laughter, everyone around them turned. "You didn't read that in a text book," he said.

"Worked, didn't it?" Oh man she did not need these memories. Strolling back to that little garage apartment after a couple margaritas to mellow them out. That lumpy bed that was too short for Dylan's 6'2" frame.

She made the mistake of looking into his eyes. He knew exactly where her thoughts were. And his were in that same lumpy bed.

"Good times." He ran one hand down her cheek. "Very good times."

It was hot in here. She shouldn't have had the wine. Images flashed like fireworks on the fourth of July. That first night on Spring Break in Colorado when they'd met, made love in that hot tub. The intimate nights that followed in his bed. Skin against skin. Her heart had shattered when she'd had to leave Colorado, knowing she'd never see him again.

Even though they'd hardly missed a day without talking, she'd almost fainted when he'd shown up in Connecticut a few months later. The passion hadn't cooled. Then Florida and...

Shake it off.

She cleared her throat. "We should probably get back and rescue your mom."

Chapter Twelve

The temperature outside had dropped during dinner. Jordan rubbed her hands together. It was going to be a chilly ride home.

Dylan held his leather jacket out for her to slip into and then pulled a thick hooded sweatshirt out of the compartment on the bike and tugged it over his head. They hadn't settled anything, but at least they were having conversations without fighting and they'd talked about the kids.

Once they got moving, the wind cut through her and her fingers felt like ice. He took her hands and slipped them beneath his sweatshirt, between it and his tee. His body heat penetrated through his thin cotton tee shirt. The scent of Dylan filled her nostrils. Even with the chill, she wasn't ready for the ride to end. She was relaxed, possibly for the first time since that early pregnancy test had come back positive.

Too soon, Dylan pulled the motorcycle into the garage, dismounted and took Jordan's hand. The house was quiet and dark, with the exception of the fireplace. And Bob Seger playing on the stereo. Had Daisy discovered that Seger was playing the first time Dylan and Jordan danced? But no sign of Daisy or the twins. Dylan helped Jordan out of his leather jacket and hung it by the back door along with his sweatshirt.

Jordan went to make sure the kids were asleep. Both out like a light. Tristan's little bottom up in the air and Trevor smacking his thumb. One of these days she needed to break him from that habit.

She tiptoed back into the family room. Dylan hadn't bothered to turn on a light. Instead he took her hand and pulled her toward the fireplace. At first, she dug her feet in. This was not smart. But her body moved closer, curling into his arms, swaying to the seductive music, melding with him. This was Dylan. The first, the only man who'd ever felt right in her arms. Or in whose arms she'd ever felt right. The man who taught her the art of love making. She stilled. The man who in anger had told her that if she didn't want to be here, to leave.

And he'd do it again, had done it once already, just since she and the boys had arrived.

She should pull out of his arms. Call it a night. Go to her room.

But the firelight flickered off the planes of his face, accenting those high cheek bones and that square jaw.

She shivered, remembering the first day they'd met. The smoky little bar in the ski lodge where they'd danced to Seger after a long day of snow mobiling. And later the steam rising off the bubbling, hot tub. The first time she and Dylan had made love...

Her hand trembled as she ran her palm down the stubble, knowing the danger. Intoxicatingly masculine. In the wee hours of the morning, naïve Jordan had reveled in the uncharacteristic wanton freedom of following the most alluring man she'd ever laid eyes on into the hot tub. She'd known him less than eighteen hours. The steam had surrounded them in a hazy, mystical cocoon as Dylan closed the distance. His face slowly coming into focus. The ecstasy of his practiced hands on her skin. The sensation of exploring every inch of his chest. And the penetrating caress from those lips, so strong and gentle.

She opened her eyes and stared into the dusty green depth of the father of her children's eyes, running her hand down the curve of Dylan's back to his tight denim-covered butt. Her gaze lowered to that sensuous mouth as a magnetic force pulled her up on tip toe to taste his lips. So, so familiar.

Dylan returned the kiss then nuzzled into her neck. She tilted her head back to give him better access, lost track of the music as one song melded into the next. They were hardly moving. She could feel Dylan's breath in her hair, his heart beating against hers. Wearing the high-heeled boots, she fit his height, still not as tall, but a good match, body part to body part.

She should push away. But his lips took possession, throbbing and demanding. Her hand moved to keep a distance between them, but instead fisted into the hair at his nape and tugged him tighter.

She closed her eyes, enjoying his hands on her bottom, gently urging her hips against his. Reacquainting herself with the feel of his chest and those wide shoulders, the muscles. The strength. She trembled as his hands dove beneath her sweater and roamed over her bare skin. Hot, warm, gentle. Dylan didn't have to actually touch her to hold her close, he just used--Dylan. A magical alluring force surrounded the man, drew her against him, even if he wasn't touching her. But he was touching her. And her him.

Suddenly his warmth was stolen away as he tugged her sweater over her head. Then his lips were on her neck, the top of her breast, just above her bra. His mouth closed over her nipple through the lace. Lowering her bra strap, she guided his mouth to where she craved it. He didn't fight. He should've. She should've, but she didn't. Being with Dylan was too right, too comfortable, too familiar.

* * *

Dylan felt Jordan grasp the bottom of his tee shirt and ease it over his head. She tossed it on the floor beside her sweater. He let out a breath, then ran his hand up her back and unclasped her bra, adding it to the growing pile of clothes in front of the fire. Hot skin to hot skin.

Her breasts fascinated him. The extra fullness felt perfect in his hand.

God he'd missed her. When he and Jordan were together, the world was in balance. Although he knew she'd leave again at the first bump in the road, when she was in his arms he couldn't worry about that.

He needed her in his bed, and he needed her there now, tonight. And from the way she was raining kisses across his chest, she was as eager as he was. A log gave way and shattered into sparks, and Seger sang on. No doubt that his mom had set the CD player to repeat because *Accomp'ny Me* had played twice, but when *We've Got Tonight* cranked up, Dylan's resistance shut down.

Bending, he scooped Jordan up and stumbled toward his bedroom. She still felt perfect in his arms. Slowly he lowered her onto the bed, but in order to get her out of those sexy black jeans, he first had to figure how to get those ridiculous high-heeled boots off. They clung to her calves like a second skin.

Jordan lay back, bent her knee and effortlessly tugged off one boot, then the other. Before the second one clunked against the wood floor, Dylan had her back in his arms and went to work on her jeans. Their arms tangled as she tugged off his. And time rolled back. She was soft and feminine in black lace panties. Sweet and sexy. Aggressive as she nibbled at his nipple and submissive as she adjusted her body beneath him. The past couple years vaporized. This was Jordan, his wonderful, passionate soul mate.

Rolling him over, she straddled him. He just wanted to be inside her, but it was still a turn-on to anticipate her next move. Her hands roamed over his body, as her expression became hazy and soft. Her eyes closed and she sighed, then she opened them and devoured his body with smoldering kisses. She embraced his shoulders, and then slid her hands slowly up to his neck and ran her thumb around his jaw. She seemed determined to touch every inch of his body and that would take way too long.

When she trailed a fingertip around the edge of his lips, he sucked her finger inside. He grabbed protection out of the bedside drawer. She nibbled her lip as she waited, then lowered herself onto his body. But she was taking things way too slow.

He flipped her over and took control. She could have it her way next time, but his body had waited too long for this. No woman had ever been able to bring him to the point of no return with just a little kitten sigh, a sigh so soft she didn't even seem to realize she made it. But she did it every time. She dug her fingers into his back and moved with him. Had they ever truly been apart?

* * *

Jordan lay snuggled against Dylan's chest, running a slender finger around his nipple. "Do you remember the first night we made love?"

First night? He remembered the entire day. Spring break and he'd been working as a snow mobile guide in Colorado. They'd told him he was going to love the group that day. He'd walked in that morning and been greeted by eight bubbly college coeds. Well, seven bubbly ones and Jordan.

"I remember it cost me fifty bucks to pay the night clerk to make sure we weren't disturbed when we snuck into the resort hot tub."

She flattened her palm against his chest. "That hot water was heaven after bouncing along on those snow mobiles."

"Helluva day."

She looked deep into his eyes. "So you still maintain that the only reason you singled me out from the other girls was because I ignored you?"

He raised an eyebrow. "Never could resist a challenge."

She pushed off his chest. "So if I'd flirted and talked to you like all the others, you might have gone with Hailey or Courtney or..."

In one move he rolled her onto her back and came gently down on top of her, kissing her deep and long. "Once I saw you I don't even remember there being other girls. Then late that night when the jukebox at that little club cranked up Seger and you melted in my arms, I knew I had to have you."

Rubbing her nose against his, she grinned. "But a hot tub?"

"It had to be special." God, he'd looked across that steamy hot tub at a vision that most men didn't have the imagination to even dream up. Innocent and gorgeous. Melting snowflakes glistened in her dark hair. The fancy lights had rotated through the water and reflected in her golden brown eyes like a kaleidoscope.

"Oh, Dylan." She wrapped her arm around his waist.

Not a day had passed since that night that Jordan Harris hadn't crossed his mind. He ran a hand down her side. Some good, others not so much, but the memories had become more vivid with time.

Including the day she'd walked out on him.

* * *

Dylan opened his eyes, blew a strand of Jordan's hair out of his face and squinted at the sun coming through the blinds. Jordan's dark hair, though shorter than the last time she'd been in his bed, still looked damned sexy fanned across his chest. But how did it get to be morning without the boys waking up? They were awake at the crack of dawn, if they even made it through the night.

The aroma of coffee wafted into the room along with some sort of cinnamon bread. He stretched his left leg, tingling from the weight of Jordan's leg thrown across his thigh. Adjusting his head on the pillow, he watched Jordan slowly wake. First her eyes fluttered, not quite opening. Then her fingers fisted, unfortunately digging into his chest in the process, but he let it pass, enjoying her morning ritual. She stretched and yawned, then came alert. The most fun was watching her face as she realized where she was. She jerked her head upward and met his gaze, as if she thought she might slide out of bed and away before he woke up.

"Good morning." He smiled.

She eased to a sitting position, clutching the sheet over her breasts. "Umm, good morning." Her gaze darted around the room, but he had no idea what she expected to find.

She scooted off the bed, dragging the sheet with her. "Where are my clothes?" When he didn't answer, she grimaced. "In the living room."

"Along with half of mine. It's fine, Jordan."

She looked like a bride as she traipsed to the closet, the white sheet trailing behind her. "I'm borrowing this shirt."

Nodding, he cocked his head and enjoyed the view of her bare backside as she dropped the sheet and slipped into his plaid flannel shirt. As she buttoned it, she peered through the bathroom toward the twins' room. "I don't think they're in there."

"That would be my guess as they haven't bounded in here to wake us up."

"Oh my gosh, what is your mom going to think? She'll know we...well..." She jabbed her fingers through her hair. "Maybe she's got the boys outside or in her room and I can sneak back to my bedroom."

Sitting on the side of the bed, he grinned at her flustered state. "I'm sure she knows where you slept and is congratulating herself."

Jordan held up a pair of jeans and tossed them his way, searching for hers. "The boys could wander in any second."

Something told him that his nakedness bothered her more than it would male toddlers. He thrust his legs into his jeans. Not finding her own jeans, Jordan took off out of the room.

He gave chase, stumbling over Sam in the doorway. "Where you going so fast?" He asked, still zipping his jeans.

Jordan peered around the corner of the hall and darted across the living room.

Dylan dodged a toy fire truck, distracted a split second only to look up and realize Jordan had stopped. His bare feet stuck to the wood floor, propelling him into her. Grabbing her shoulders, he barely kept them both from doing a face plant.

He followed the direction of her wide-eyed stare to the kitchen where his mom was busy with the twins. Rusty sat at the bar, hands wrapped around a coffee mug.

"Bout time you two sleepy heads woke up. Coffee is on. I made cinnamon rolls," Daisy said, placing sippy cups in front of the kids.

It was all he could do to keep a straight face. Jordan seemed chagrined, especially with Rusty in the house. Daisy hummed as she danced about the kitchen, but Rusty didn't look as pleased.

"Uh, thanks." Jordan tugged at the hem of Dylan's shirt, which seemed silly since it reached half way to her knees. "I'll just get dressed." Spinning on her heel, she stalked from the kitchen.

The twins sat at their table, still wearing their fuzzy sleepers and up to their elbows in gooey white icing from the cinnamon rolls.

"Papa." Tristan raced toward him, reaching out his grimy little hands.

How could he resist the sound of his boy calling him Papa? Grabbing him around the waist, Dylan lifted him and kissed his forehead, the only part of him that wasn't covered with icing. The kid still somehow managed to smack Dylan's bare chest with a sticky hand. "Daisy make you a good breakfast?"

Dylan held the kid a safe distance away from him and sailed him through the air like a plane. As soon as he landed him in his chair, Tristan pulled his plate toward him and wrapped his arms around it to guard his food from his ever hungry brother.

"Yum," Trevor said.

Dylan kissed the top of Trev's blond curls. "It smells yum."

Daisy handed Dylan a damp cloth. "You might want to wash their hands."

Dylan snagged the cloth and swiped the sticky goo out of his chest hair. "Ehhh, let them finish clogging their pores with icing and then I'll toss them in the tub and hose 'em down."

Daisy wiped her hands on a dish towel, stood on tiptoe and kissed his cheek. "Did you and Jordan have a nice dinner?"

He narrowed an eye at her. Quite a nice dinner indeed, but then she knew that. She'd engineered it. "Yeah, Mom. It was...good."

Dylan didn't miss Rusty's raised eyebrows. The hell of it was, his cousin was dead on. Unless Dylan was a masochist, he should run as fast as he could in the opposite direction.

"Morning, Rusty."

"Mornin'. Figured you could use a hand mending that fence in the back forty."

"Cool."

Jordan re-entered the living room, scooped last night's clothes up from in front of the fireplace and high-tailed it back to her room. As if Daisy didn't already know what had happened between them.

Jordan rushed back into the kitchen, rubbing her hands down the front of her fresh jeans. She ignored Dylan and focused on

Daisy. "Thanks for making them breakfast, but I can take it from here."

"I'm loving every minute of this," Daisy said.

Not even attempting to hide a grin, Dylan poured a cup of coffee and grabbed a cinnamon roll. "You got the boys? I'm already getting a late start. Those chores aren't gonna get done on their own."

She gave Rusty a sideways glance, then nodded at Dylan.

He jumped in and out of the shower then reached in the drawer for clean underwear. Rummaging to the back, he pulled out the small box he'd put there two years ago, along with the cryptic note Jordan had stuck on the bathroom mirror the day she'd left. He clutched the ring and studied the bed, still rumpled from their lovemaking. Where the hell were they supposed to go from here?

Chapter Thirteen

Jordan breathed a sigh of relief when Rusty and Dylan finally left the house. She needed time to recover her composure. Okay, so she shouldn't have slept with Dylan. But that didn't explain why his cousin didn't like her. Didn't want her here and especially not with Dylan. The closed-minded cowboy hadn't even said good morning.

But then, neither had she.

She wasn't sure what she expected from Dylan's mother after the night before, but Daisy acted like nothing had changed. She sang her way through the morning, playing with the boys and cleaning up here and there. Today's music choice was Country. And not the typical somebody done somebody wrong country. The newer, sexier, throbbing country. Jordan wasn't sure who the artists were, but their lyrics hit a little too close to home.

Daisy hadn't uttered a single syllable about Jordan being in Dylan's room this morning. Not even when in the process of digging one of Trevor's Legos out from beneath the leather sofa, she pulled out Jordan's black lace bra. The one she should have known better than to wear when she'd put it on last evening.

Completely mortified, Jordan felt the flush from her face ooze down her neck and continue to her toes.

Still dressed in hot pink and orange striped PJs, Daisy handed Trevor the toy, Jordan the bra and never missed a beat to some guy on the stereo asking a girl if he still turned her on.

Daisy Zimmerman added an entire new level to the term free spirit. Jordan could only imagine how this zany, petite little wild woman had knocked straight laced, bull rider Mac McKeon off his scuffed cowboy boots and kept him off balance for the next thirty years.

And the result of their love was Dylan, a mix of both parents. Raised on the ranch with horses and chores and a dad who taught him the love of animals and ranch life. With California trips and visits from a free-spirited mother who taught him to love life, music and adventure. And to follow his dreams.

Jordan stopped in front of the shelf of photos and searched for a particular family photo she remembered. Picking up the silly snapshot of Dylan, Daisy and Mac on the beach in California, suddenly pieces fell into place.

Long straight hair flying wildly around her face, a beaming Daisy wore a fluorescent pink and green bikini and a sultry grin. Mac on the other hand, looked like someone had cut his silhouette out of a rodeo magazine and pasted it on a beach with a glue stick. Wearing only jeans and a cowboy hat, with one knee bent, he was leaning against a boulder in the edge of the surf. Without a shirt and exhibiting those insanely wide shoulders, he bore an uncanny resemblance to his now grown son.

Jordan's eyes focused on the young Dylan in the photo. Probably seven or eight years old, wearing an obnoxiously bright floral swimsuit that Daisy had no doubt bought, and holding a fluorescent orange sand pail and shovel. Dylan was grinning, but looked confused. Like he wasn't sure which parent's lead to follow. A silly fun loving mommy? Or a tough, obviously out of his element daddy?

Having been raised by these two, Dylan would make an interesting case study. But it'd take someone more advanced in psychoanalysis than Jordan. Certainly not textbook. There was enough depth and conflict in his past to write an entire book entitled, *Dylan, The Free Spirited Cowboy*. Just by the pictures on this one shelf, she could list the Table of Contents: Lonely Little Boy, High School Quarterback, Air Force Mechanic, Hells Angel, Free Spirit, Hot Headed Cowboy, Hard Working Rancher, and Horse Whisperer. She blinked...Father...Lover Extraordinaire.

Every single thing Dylan undertook he did to perfection, trying to earn his father's approval. Not love. He'd known he was loved by both parents, yet according to him, he'd never quite fit in with either. Never believed he'd measured up to either parent's expectations. Maybe because his mom had left him when he was a child and moved back to California. Or because his father had become an alcoholic. At a young age, Dylan had been forced to take responsibility for the ranch and in many ways, become the parent to his father. Whatever the reasoning, Dylan McKeon was one of a kind.

She ran a finger down the snapshot. How could a man so difficult to understand be so easy to fall in love with?

Twice.

* * *

Dylan's silence at dinner confused Jordan even more. He was pleasant and helped feed the kids, then carted them off for their baths. They'd fallen into the routine of Dylan bathing them and Jordan reading the bedtime story. Actually, she understood Dylan enjoying bathing them. A lot of work and you always ended up drenched, but still the kids had so much fun, you couldn't help but get into their excitement.

Jordan helped Daisy clean the kitchen, then they retired to the sofa. Watching the door for two pajama clad little boys, Jordan surfed the TV channels, but there wasn't anything on worth watching.

Daisy opted for country music videos. She grinned. "The only time I listen to this music is when I'm here, but it just goes with the house."

One thing Jordan could say about country music was that the artists had certainly gotten better looking. The guy singing wore a pair of tight faded jeans, a black shirt and had a deep sexy voice. The lyrics were still a bit melancholy, but not a twinge of twang. "It does fit."

Daisy perused the young singer and wiggled her eyebrows. "I wouldn't kick him out of bed."

In her wildest dreams, Jordan could never imagine her mother admit to noticing some guy's looks, much less making such an outlandish statement. Problem was when Jordan looked at the way the soft denim cupped the guy's butt, all she could think was that he didn't hold a candle to the man bathing her boys. Speaking of which, had they drowned?

"I'm going to check whether Dylan needs help fishing the kids out."

Daisy's gaze never strayed from the TV screen. "Yell if you need me."

Walking into the kids' bedroom, Jordan inhaled the scent of baby powder. Wearing his green frog sleeper, Tristan smiled as he came toward her, like he had some wonderful secret. He pulled a red rose from behind his back and handed it to her. Taking the flower, she smiled and gave him a kiss. "Thanks, sweetie."

Her eyes searched out Dylan as he huddled with Trevor on the far side of the room. He urged the boy forward, but Trevor didn't seem as excited about whatever was going on as his brother had been. Still, he ambled toward her and thrust a velvet jewelry box into her hand. Her gut wrenched, but she managed a hug. "Thank you, Trevor."

She stood and faced Dylan. He cradled one boy against each leg, but his gray-green eyes bore through her. "Let's do this thing right. Let's make a family together for our kids. Stay here. Marry me."

Her heart skipped a couple beats. Then she searched his face. He looked determined, but not in love. His words only confirmed it. He was doing this for the kids, not because he loved her.

Not even bothering to open the box, she shoved it into Dylan's hand. She'd die a slow death, knowing that the only reason he wanted her here was because of their children. She loved him too much to live like that. Eventually, she'd wither away like her mother had. "Wanting to make a home for our children is no reason to get married. We'd make each other miserable. Just like before. And then we'd make *them* miserable."

The look of devastation on his face was almost her undoing, but he didn't exactly rush to assure her that he loved her more than the moon and stars. He just stared at her like she was the most unreasonable, horrible person in the world. "Miserable?"

"I can't do this, Dylan." Before she started blubbering like a lovesick schoolgirl, she turned and raced to her room. She had to have a few minutes to get control. *Hold it together. Don't cry!*

The man didn't even knock, just opened the door and stormed into her bedroom. "You always said you hated it when I let my emotions rule my brain. So now I've tried bare bones logic and you're the one acting emotional."

"I'm not emotional." But the pounding in her chest beat out a different story. "Where are the boys?"

"Mom has 'em. Look at me, dammit!"

"Don't yell at me." Stay calm. She just needed him to give this up and leave. No way could she spend nights in his arms knowing that he didn't love her.

Blowing out a breath, he looked up at the ceiling, then back at her. He fisted his hands on his hips. "We've been through some rough times. Most likely there will be more. But we both love the boys and I think the best thing we can do for them is to get married and raise them together. Give them stability."

Stability? How stable could a one sided marriage be? "You just want to raise your kids full time, and in the process, you get a bed partner."

"We both would." That telltale left eye of his narrowed. "I distinctly remember you unzipping my jeans last night."

Heat spread up her neck to her cheeks. The passion was still there, no doubt. Was there hope? "Maybe I could just stay a little longer. See how it goes." Not smart, but it made tons more sense than rushing into a marriage. Maybe in time he'd grow to love her again, trust her.

"So you're still afraid of commitment?"

She blew out a breath. "Like you said, there's been a lot of water under the bridge. We shouldn't rush into anything. Give it time."

"Not good enough. I don't want to yank our kids half way across the country between parents who can't make up their minds. I've been there. It sucks. No wishy-washy, let's see what happens. We make a commitment to ourselves and to them to make this family work. Sign our names on a marriage license, rings on our fingers, parents and children with the same last name."

"Oh, like my parents? They stayed together and made each other, and me, miserable. They didn't quit. They just kept on until there was no life left. A marriage license is no guarantee. Not when you don't trust me."

"Why the hell should I? You already left once when things got tough. Guarantee or not, I want your signature on the dotted line promising you won't do it again."

Her chest threatened to cave in from the void left from the words he wasn't saying. He'd never trust her, marriage or no marriage. He'd never love her like he had before. "That wouldn't solve anything."

"You're hedging because you know you'll bolt at the first sign of trouble, just like before." He gritted his teeth. "So if you don't want to be here, why prolong the torture? Get out now! Tonight! Go home. I'll drive you to the airport."

"Every time we argue, that's your response. Tell me to leave. Who's afraid of commitment, Dylan?" Her eyes stung with tears, but she met his cold stare, eyeball to eyeball, even though her body threatened to shut down. They'd had this same argument. Only the first time she'd left. Her girlish dreams shattered.

"This is bullshit! We're both victims of our upbringings, but you're too hardheaded to learn from that and make a better life for our kids. And to add insult to injury, you want to shift that blame to me. How the hell is that supposed to work? You left and when you found out you were pregnant, didn't bother to tell me. And when I found out, you accused me of not being a good father, which still makes my blood boil. And I was still willing to get married and work at it. You obviously aren't. But my sons will have my name."

Before she could respond, he stomped out of the room, then the back door slammed and within seconds, the Harley roared to life.

Perfect. Maybe he'd run the stupid macho machine off a bridge. Her body shook beyond trembling into downright vibrating and her knees buckled. Grasping the side of the bed, she slid to the floor. She clutched her knees to her chest, threw her head back and let the tears flow.

The last time she'd lived here, Dylan had gotten into an argument with his father and roared away on that damn motorcycle in a cloud of dust and gravel. Jordan had lay in bed unable to sleep for hours before he finally returned. She could still distinctly remember how he'd smelled, almost like the wind. She'd kissed away his pain and they'd made love until the sun came up.

But tonight would not end romantically.

Willing? Dylan had said willing as if he was making a sacrifice by marrying her.

She had to pull herself together and check on the kids. If they heard their father yelling, they'd be upset. They weren't accustomed to raised voices. But as she listened to the roar of the Harley fade away, the only sound from the rest of the house was some male country singer wanting a booty call. How could anyone enjoy that melodramatic country BS? Earth shattering sex was just one element of what was important for the long haul. She swiped at her eyes and tried to figure out what she was feeling. Grabbing her cell phone off the bureau, she went into the living room. Daisy and the boys were stretched out on a pallet in front of the fireplace playing with toys.

"You okay?" Daisy asked.

Jordan shrugged. She shouldn't ask, but Daisy obviously had witnessed Dylan storming out. "Do you think he's going to Zoe?"

"Possibly. I'd rather he go to her than kill himself racing around the countryside on that motorcycle."

Jordan took a deep breath. "Yeah."

Shoving her arms into her jacket, Jordan glanced at Sam, lying by the door to the garage, head resting on his front paws and looking at her with those sad puppy dog eyes like she was a monster. "It wasn't my fault. I didn't tell him to leave," she said, then rubbed her eyes. "I'm talking to a dog."

Sam didn't change expressions, just remained by the door awaiting his master's return.

She stepped out onto the back porch and dialed Cara. If anyone could help her make sense of this, it was her mentor. After all, she'd talked Jordan through surviving Dylan McKeon the first time. Night after miserable night.

She didn't even say hello when Cara answered. "He did it, Cara."

"Hello, Jordan." There was a slight pause. "He being Dylan, I presume."

"He proposed." Jordan felt tears stream down her cheeks. "He got all rational and I don't know how to deal with a rational Dylan. No mention of love or romance in his proposal."

"Whoa!" Jordan could visualize Cara sitting forward and pushing her wire rimmed glasses up on her nose. "Dylan proposed? What did you say?"

"The most romantic man ever just delivered the least romantic proposal anyone could come up with. He wants his kids full time and he's willing to take me in the bargain. I turned him down, then he told me to leave. Just like he always does. He..." Jordan swiped her tears on her jacket sleeve.

"Come on Jordan, you're smart enough to figure this out."

"Yeah. He's rejecting me. Chasing me away. He did it the first time we were together and this is the second time since I've been back that he's told me to get out."

"And?"

Jordan pulled the front of her jacket together, then realized it was Dylan's jacket. The leather mixed with the musky scent of Dylan. A fresh flow of tears pooled behind her eyes and trickled down her face. "And he's testing me."

Cara sighed. "Think about that little boy whose mother left him. He expects you to leave so he's seeing how far he can push to prove that you're like her."

"And I failed the first time. But he didn't come after me. If he'd loved me, he would have."

"Would he?"

Jordan shook her head. "I don't know."

"Now that you've been under the same roof for over a week, are the old feelings really dead?"

She couldn't answer that. She knew the answer, but she couldn't make the words come out of her mouth for fear of having to actually face the reality.

"Jordan?"

"I can't imagine loving another man besides Dylan McKeon. But we're opposites."

"Have you had sex?"

"I defy any red blooded woman to resist the man when she's the focus of his attention. Dylan..."

"So the passion hasn't cooled?"

"Cara," Jordan whispered. "I destroyed his trust. I can't even blame him. But the thing I loved about him was his passion and his emotion. Both things that were dead in me. But now, he just wants to give the boys a stable home."

"Thinking about his children and putting them first is a good thing."

"He doesn't love me!" Jordan took a deep breath. "Even when I all but asked him, he never mentioned the word love. And Dylan always told me he loved me. He'd look straight through me with those intense eyes and make sure I understood how much he loved me."

Silence.

More silence.

"Talk to me, Cara."

"It may not work, Jordan. Possibly in this instance, there is just too much that's happened for you two to overcome. You may be setting yourself up for disappointment to believe he could ever get back to the way he felt before. Are you prepared for that?"

This wasn't right. This was not the way this conversation was supposed to go. Cara was supposed to tell her what to do. To assure her that she could fix this. To tell her that as long as she loved him, there was always a way, always hope. "I don't know."

Jordan ended the conversation and dialed her mom. Mom wouldn't ask questions, wouldn't dig too deep.

Mom listened without speaking as Jordan poured out the whole tale, one more time.

"Mom?"

"I'm worried about you. You don't sound at all well. What if I come there? Fly home with you and the twins next week?"

"I'd like that very much." Jordan sniffed. "I'm worried about me too, Mom."

* * *

Jordan wasn't surprised when Rusty returned to the house with Dylan for lunch the next day. She'd still been awake at two in the morning when Rusty's pickup had followed Dylan's motorcycle into the drive. At least it hadn't been Zoe's truck. The two men had stood outside for a long time, then Dylan had left the house this morning before the sun came up. He couldn't have gotten more than a couple hours sleep.

Daisy flitted around the kitchen, making tuna sandwiches for everyone. Dylan played with the twins and even helped feed them, but for all the attention he paid Jordan, she might as well have not been there.

"Dylan, I talked to my mom last night. She wants to fly in at the end of the week and help me with the twins on the flight home."

He frowned. "Your idea or hers?"

"Hers. Does it matter?"

"Sounds like it's been decided." Dylan put his plate in the dishwasher and grinned at the kids. "You guys want to go horseback riding with Papa and Rusty?"

Trevor's eyes sparkled. "Hosey."

Seeing his brother's excitement, Tristan grinned. "Me."

Jordan shook her head. "I don't think they're old enough to ride horses. And they're just getting over colds."

He zipped Trevor into his blue windbreaker. "It's seventy degrees and they aren't going to be riding alone. They'll be in my lap."

Jordan grabbed a sweatshirt off the peg as Dylan zipped Tristan into his jacket. "I'm coming along."

"We've got it covered," Rusty assured her, taking Trevor's hand. "We're going to have a guy's afternoon."

Jordan wasn't about to let the boys go on a guy's afternoon with horses that outweighed them by about a million tons. "You don't mind if I tag along, do you?"

"Suit yourself. Just didn't think you liked horses," Dylan said.

She started to say more, but any objection would sound whiney. Dylan would not let them get hurt, but the boys were so little.

"Get your hats, guys. Man needs a hat to ride a horse."

The boys raced into their room and returned wearing the cowboy hats that Zoe had bought them.

"Ready to go now." Tristan said, stringing together more syllables than he'd ever said.

Dylan took each twin by the hand. "So you're ready to ride Papa's horse? His name is Cinder."

Okay, technically Cinder was Dylan's now, but Jordan remembered his father's huge stallion. Maybe it was the glossy midnight black coat along with the size, but she'd always been leery of the stallion. "Dylan, couldn't they ride with you on one of the smaller animals?"

"Cinder's trained. They'll be safer." He winked. "Besides, I'll be driving."

Rusty rolled his eyes.

She grimaced, remembering how Dylan had kidded her use of the word driving a horse the first time he'd attempted to get her on one. She did not appreciate the taunt in front of Rusty who already thought she was a moron.

The second time Trevor stopped to pick up a rock from the road, Dylan hoisted him onto his shoulders. He placed the hat that had fallen off back atop Trevor's blond curls and picked up the pace. Rusty swung Tristan up in the same fashion. Jordan followed behind, seething. Sam happily trotted along bringing up the rear.

The huge black horse was saddled and in the stall when they arrived. Dylan handed Trevor to Jordan. "Hold him and I'll take Tristan around the corral first."

Sam flopped down on a blanket in the patch of sun in the corner for an afternoon nap.

Everything went fine as Dylan held Tristan and introduced him to Cinder, showing him how to rub the horse's nose. "Feel how soft."

"Soft." Tristan nodded and stroked the nose, his hand looking tiny and dangerously close to the horse's mouth and teeth, but Cinder stood patiently. Dylan held out his hand with a sugar cube. The horse nuzzled his palm and took the cube. "You want to give him one?"

Tristan shook his head back and forth, clinging to Dylan's neck. It was fine with Jordan that he wasn't willing to get too close to the mouth.

Dylan handed him to Rusty, then mounted the horse. But when Rusty started to lift Tristan up, the boy grabbed him around the neck and wailed. "Mama!"

Jordan sat Trevor down and reached over the fence for Tristan. Rusty didn't immediately give him to her. Instead, he patted the boy's back and tried to comfort him. "It's okay. Cinder just wants to be friends."

"Give him to me!" Her son was afraid and needed his mommy.

Dylan pushed his hat back and nodded toward Jordan. Rusty placed the baby in her arms. Dismounting, Dylan said something to Rusty, but Jordan couldn't hear over Tristan's hiccups. Dylan squatted beside Trevor. "You wanna meet Cinder?"

Trevor beamed. He'd always been fascinated with any animal. "Me go."

Dylan picked him up and went through the same routine, only this time letting him spend more time getting comfortable. Jordan's heart stopped when Trevor fed the horse a sugar cube right out of his tiny hand.

Dylan lifted him into the saddle, never taking his hands away from the boy's waist. Trevor grinned and looked very much like a miniature cowboy, right down to the cowboy hat. "Go."

Dylan handed him to Rusty while he remounted. When Rusty handed him up, Trevor leaned back against his Papa's chest and smiled in contentment. Dylan took it slow for a couple laps around the pen. "You ready to go check out the stream on the other side of the field? When you get bigger we'll go fishing."

Trevor continued to grin like a kid on an amusement park ride.

Rusty opened the gate and Dylan slowly walked the horse into the larger field and away from Jordan. Tristan stopped crying, his gaze glued to his brother.

Rusty leaned against the fence. "If you hadn't jumped to his rescue so quick, he'd have been fine."

So he knew more about her child than she did? "Don't interfere with the way I raise my children."

"Dylan's children too," Rusty clarified, retrieving Tristan's hat and dusting it off on his jeans leg. "He knows what he's doing. He won't let them get hurt." His tone was even more condescending than his words.

"You don't need to remind me that they're Dylan's kids."

"Yeah, well." He shrugged.

"Yeah, well, what?"

Rusty turned from the fence. "What kind of woman doesn't even see fit to tell a guy she's pregnant?"

"Are you questioning their paternity?"

Rusty snorted. "I know they're his and I know he loves them."

"So it's me you're questioning? Come on, Rusty. Let's get it out in the open. We both know you don't like me."

"No, I don't. You're like poison for Dylan." Rusty scowled.

Jordan gulped. "Poison? Because you think Zoe would be a better partner?"

"You bet." He nodded. "They get along like they're one and the same. They don't fight and she's up front and honest with him, something you've never been. You damn near destroyed him the first time around."

Tristan laid his head on her shoulder and clutched her hair. Destroyed? "I realize I didn't handle things well, but aren't you over-reacting?"

Rusty closed the distance between them and glared. "Why the hell do you think he no longer drinks?"

She shook her head. "Because his father was an alcoholic."

"Convincing yourself of that's more palatable than facing reality, huh? He's too smart to let some bimbo do the same thing to him Daisy did to Uncle Mac."

Jordan gulped, but before she could defend herself, Cinder loped back into the corral. Rusty turned from her and grinned as he took Trevor from Dylan. "You have fun, buddy?"

Trevor's little head bobbed up and down and his eyes sparkled in pure male exuberance. "Go fast."

Dylan focused those gray-green eyes on her. "Probably best to wait until another day for Tristan?"

She studied Dylan in light of the argument with Rusty. "Yes. I'll take them back to the house."

Dylan dismounted and handed Trevor a brush for the horse. "As soon as he gets sleepy, I'll bring him inside."

"It's past time for their naps. I'll take them both."

His eyes narrowed. "Have it your way."

Chapter Fourteen

Dylan unstrapped the saddle, sneaking a glance at Jordan's cute little denim-covered ass as she headed to the house. He placed the saddle aside and turned just in time to catch the brunt of Rusty's right hook as it cracked into his cheek.

His back slammed into the fence, but he rebounded and landed his fist into Rusty's jaw.

Rusty grabbed his jaw with one hand, but his right fist was poised for the next punch. Cinder pawed the ground with his front hoof and moved out of range. Sam stood a foot away, on alert.

"What the hell are you doing?" Dylan's cheek throbbed and he took a step toward Rusty, bracing himself to foil the next blow.

Rusty took one step back, but didn't drop his stance. "What are you doing, Dylan?"

"You hit me!" Dylan stared him down.

"Remember that night I hauled your shit-faced self home and you were all maudlin over Jordan? After I poured half a pot of coffee down you, it finally penetrated your thick skull that you were following the same self-destructive path as Uncle Mac. You told me to knock you on your ass if you ever so much as mentioned Jordan Harris' name."

Not one of his finer moments. Dylan unclenched his fist and massaged his bruised cheekbone. "Yeah, but the twins add a new wrinkle. I'd hoped for once she'd listen to reason. She's a trained counselor and the one thing she's always claimed to be is logical." Dylan retrieved his hat and dusted it off on his jeans. "She's not, but she thinks she is. She's like a mechanic who can't keep his own car running."

"She's female. Counselor or otherwise, logic doesn't run in her DNA." Rusty picked up a curry brush as Cinder ventured close again.

"I just thought." Dylan ran a hand down the stallion's neck. "I mean, after the other night, I thought maybe, given that we both love the boys and want to do what's best for them, that getting married was the answer."

Rusty scoffed and held out a sugar cube to the horse. "Do you love her?"

Talk about a loaded question. "At one time I thought she was the one. God, I loved that woman. But now it's all a muddle. The cold-hearted way she left. The lies." The way she'd made love to him the other night. Her body burning against his. "She's a good mom."

"Not a good enough reason to marry her," Rusty said continuing to work on the horse. "So, how you holding up?"

Dylan cocked an eyebrow and picked up another brush. "Other than feeling like I've been rode hard and put up wet, I'm fine."

Rusty worked a burr out of Cinder's tail. "Well, whatever you decide, the only thing to consider is what's best for you and your kids. She's already proven that she can't be trusted."

* * *

Long after Rusty left, Dylan hung out in the barn prolonging his return to the house. He wanted to avoid seeing Jordan as long as possible. To forget he'd ever loved her.

He turned Cinder out to pasture and let the new horse loose in the round pen while he tended to the chores. After a couple slow laps around the pen, the animal stood on the far side and tentatively watched him. Dylan held his stare a few seconds and let his drop. Let him win this round.

He mucked out the stalls and put down fresh hay, leaving the gate open to give the horse the freedom to roam back into the stables if he wanted. As he oiled down Cinder's saddle, he caught movement out of the corner of his eye, but he continued the chore, not making eye contact with the rescued horse.

The horse would take a couple steps closer, then stop and wait, watch Dylan. Today, not sure who or what to trust anymore, Dylan felt a strong kinship with the abused animal.

Maybe he could just throw a sleeping bag down out here. Take a night off from Jordan. Sam looked comfortable enough stretched out on his blanket with all four feet in the air as he snored. The dog hadn't been more than hollering distance from him since he'd gotten home at two this morning. He'd tripped over the silly animal when he'd stumbled out of bed three hours later.

Bunking out here over the next few days actually sounded like a good plan. There was a coffee pot on the counter and he could grab his fishing pole and with any luck, catch dinner out of the creek.

He could avoid Jordan's mother. Not that the woman had ever uttered more than a dozen words to him in the entire time he'd known her.

But as desperate as he was to avoid Jordan and her soon-to-be-arriving mother, the desire to spend every second of the time left with the boys won out. Their stay was already more than half over. He refused to let Jordan ruin it for him. He'd just stay the hell out of Jordan's proximity as much as possible.

The rescued horse took another two steps closer.

The saddle was done, but Dylan continued to rub the soft rag over it, giving the horse time to decide whether he was ready to come closer, ready to trust. One more step and he'd be within touching range. He didn't look up, just let him figure it out on his own.

A soft nose nuzzled under his arm. Gently, Dylan fished a sugar cube out of his pocket. As he held it out, the horse sniffed it and took it from his hand. Slowly, Dylan ran a hand down the golden nose. "You're with friends here, fella. Nobody's gonna hurt you."

He wished he felt the same about the woman in the house and his heart.

He continued to rub the horses nose, offered him another sugar cube. "We just gotta stick together, boy. You hungry?"

At the sound of the word hungry, Sam rolled to his feet, ears perked and tongue lolled out.

Dylan rubbed his eyes. "Yeah, I know, Sam. Time for dinner."

* * *

Jordan pulled Dylan's dad's pickup to the curb by the arrival gate outside DFW airport and searched the crowd for her mother. Tristan was asleep in the car seat and Dylan had kept Trevor home with him. The past couple days at the ranch had been strained. They needed to talk things out, but Dylan seemed to have worked out a method of spending time with the kids and ignoring her. And at this point, she didn't trust herself to carry on a conversation with him anyway.

The next couple of days were going to be grueling, but she'd survived leaving him once and she could do it again. Right? Now, because of the kids, he'd always be a part of her life. Moving past the current status between them would be challenging at best.

When her mother walked through the exit door, Jordan was so happy to see her that she almost broke down in tears. But her happiness quickly dampened when her father stepped into view. She hadn't invited him. It had been awkward enough telling Dylan that her mother was coming.

She stepped out of the truck and waved. "Mom, over here."

Both parents turned and strode toward her. Her father scrutinized the huge, ten year old, king cab pickup, but didn't comment as he heaved their two suitcases into the bed. "Will these ride okay back here?"

"They'll be fine," she said, hugging her mother and nodding toward her father.

"Dad wanted to see where the boys might be spending some time. Make sure they're in a safe environment." Mom smiled, but her voice quivered. She opened the back door and climbed in, squeezing Tristan's leg. "Oh, let me look at you. Where's your brother?"

Dad sat in the front seat.

Tristan opened his eyes and favored his grandmother with a groggy smile like he wasn't quite sure why this person was in this particular place, but happy to see her just the same.

"Trevor was asleep when it was time for me to leave so Dylan kept him."

Mom smoothed Tristan's dark curls off his forehead. "Have you had fun at the ranch?"

"Hosey!" Tristan beamed.

As they left DFW, her father leaned back. "Do we need to rent a hotel? How big is this log cabin?"

"It's a four bedroom log house." Jordan almost looked forward to her father's reaction when he saw the ranch. Though not fancy by any stretch, the house was nice and it sat on almost two-hundred acres. "But if you'd be more comfortable staying elsewhere, there are hotels in Denton."

"You don't think we'll be welcome?"

Oh, this was so like him. To try to lay the issue on Dylan when it was her father who had come uninvited. "I'm sure you'll be welcome. And you'll get to meet Dylan's mom."

Actually, she wasn't at all sure Dylan would make her father welcome. If she'd had a chance before they got in the truck, she'd have called Dylan and told him her father was here so he could have an hour to get used to the idea.

This was not going to be pretty. It might be best if they did rent a hotel for the two nights until the agreement allowed her to return home with the boys.

Lost in thought, she didn't even make small talk until she turned down the white rock road toward the house.

"He lives on a dirt road?" Her father's disdain was clear in each syllable.

Jordan took a deep breath and kept her voice level as the truck bumped across the narrow bridge that spanned the white rock creek. The foliage was beginning to paint the landscape for fall, but her father wouldn't notice the beauty. "The road is part of the ranch."

Her mother sighed. "It's very nice. Is that Dylan's house?" She pointed through the trees.

"That's the old farm house that was on the property when Mac bought it thirty years ago. Dylan's grandparents moved into it after Mac built the log house for him and Daisy. Now that his grandparents are gone, Dylan's cousin rents it."

Dylan's small herd of cows grazed in the green pasture to the east of the house, but Jordan turned the opposite direction where he was plowing the hayfield under. Her heart stopped. Trevor sat in his father's lap, looking very much at ease. She shifted the truck into park and waited for the tractor to make the corner and pull up beside the fence.

"Is that safe?" Mom asked, straining toward the window for a closer look.

"Papa," Tristan squealed, kicking his feet and fighting the car seat restraints. "Me go."

Dylan slid off the tractor and hoisted Trevor onto his shoulders. As he approached, Jordan saw that left eye narrow and realized the exact moment he spotted her dad sitting in the pickup. She held her breath as Tristan continued to squeal. "Me!"

As her father stepped out of the truck, Dylan extended his hand. "Welcome to Texas."

Dad accepted the handshake across the fence. "Thank you."

Dylan grinned at her mother. "Glad you could make the trip."

The smell of fresh tilled dirt filled her nostrils as Jordan unbuckled Tristan's car seat. "I don't think you have any choice but to let Tristan ride or he's going to bust a gut."

Dylan handed Trevor across to her and took Tristan. He didn't comment as the boy hugged Jordan's mom.

"Did you miss grandmother?" Mom asked, returning the hug.

Tristan grabbed Dylan's hand and tugged. "Go."

"We'll probably be another hour." He lifted Tristan onto his shoulders and tipped his hat. "Make yourselves at home."

Jordan let out a breath. Dylan was trying and so far, her father hadn't been rude. Maybe on Dylan's turf, Dad would curb his tendency to talk down to him.

They made their way down the tree lined road and parked in front of the house. Jordan helped her father retrieve the luggage as her mom carried Trevor.

Daisy threw open the door wearing a flowing black caftan with hot pink Hibiscus scattered across the front. She even had a pink flower pinned in her hair. How in the world would her parents react to Daisy? As sweet as the woman was, she was a bit of an airhead. With typical Daisy exuberance, she hugged first Mom and then Dad, kissing their cheeks. "Oh, I'm so tickled to finally meet you both." She grinned at Jordan. "I didn't realize your father was coming. What a wonderful surprise!"

Both her parents stood in their crisp business casual slacks and shirts, staring at Daisy like she had just descended from a spaceship.

Daisy held the door open. "Well come on in. I have a brisket in the oven for dinner whenever Dylan gets done plowing the hay under. Whatever that means."

Jordan inhaled the rich aroma of coffee blended with whatever concoction Daisy had marinated the brisket in. George Strait's mellow voice played softly on the stereo, singing something about Amarillo. Funny that she recognized country artists by their voice now. It had just sort of slipped up on her. Her parents, however, had never listened to country music in their lives.

"Oh, pardon my manners." Daisy clapped her hand to her chest. "Daisy Zimmerman, Dylan's mom."

"Franklin and Margaret Harris." Her father adjusted his glasses as Daisy squeezed his hand. "Zimmerman? You and Dylan's father were divorced?"

"Oh lordy no. Why ruin a lovely relationship with the antiquated state of matrimony?" She shook her head and handed Trevor a gooey chocolate chip cookie, her tinkling laughter filling the room.

Jordan watched her father's expression. The only one who looked more surprised, or shocked, was her mother.

Daisy herded Trevor toward the little table beside the window to eat his cookie. She held out the plate to Jordan's parents. "I just brewed a fresh pot of coffee. I prefer green tea, but Dylan and Mac love their coffee. There are also sodas."

"We'd like to take our bags to our room and wash up first, if you don't mind." Jordan could read her father's disapproval. This little tidbit just added to his arsenal against Dylan.

Jordan picked up her mom's case. "This way, Dad." She'd no more than placed the case on the bench at the foot of the guestroom bed than her father started in.

"So Dylan McKeon is a bastard just like his sons. Why does that not surprise me?"

"Dad, you're the one who insisted that I not tell Dylan I was pregnant, so..."

Margaret twisted her hands. "We shouldn't judge."

Frank Harris looked at Jordan. "I cannot imagine what you ever saw in that man."

Jordan bit her tongue and held her response.

Mom, always the peacemaker, glanced around the bedroom. "The house is very spacious."

"Mac was a big guy. He didn't like to be cramped."

"How many square feet?" her dad asked.

"I think around three-thousand, but I'm not sure." Jordan rather enjoyed the frustration on her father's face when it registered that Dylan's home was larger than his.

* * *

Even the wooden-handled steak knives wouldn't have been sharp enough to cut the tension at dinner. The two men hardly spoke, at least not to each other. Afterwards Dylan shooed everyone out of the kitchen and insisted on cleaning up. A nice gesture, even though Jordan knew that he didn't mind cleaning the kitchen nearly as much as he hated sparring with her father.

Jordan cleared the table. She needed a chance to speak to Dylan alone. As he rinsed dishes, she piled the last dish on the granite countertop. "Thanks for not making a big deal about this. I was as surprised as you when my dad showed up."

Loading the dishwasher, he didn't speak for a minute. "He's calculating the value of your half of the ranch. Why else would he have come?"

She leaned around to see Dylan's face. "I think he's checking out the environment that the kids will be in when they visit."

He straightened and met her face to face. "I wish I thought that, but even you know better. He hasn't showed either of them the slightest attention all evening."

"He loves them. He's just not demonstrative." Jordan recited the same thing her mom had always told her when she wondered why her father never hugged her or played with her. He'd seldom missed a school program and was at her graduations from high school and college. He'd made sure she had the best of whatever she needed, but he'd been emotionally unavailable.

When she looked back at Dylan, he was watching her intently. "I'm sorry for the way you were raised." Uncanny the way Dylan could always read her.

In spite of the fact that she'd convinced herself that none of that mattered now, her eyes filled with tears. Dylan's family, with all their quirks, were huggers. Mac had always hugged Dylan. Of course, Mac had been drunk more times than sober and alcohol had a way of loosening a person's inhibitions. She remembered one night after Daisy had returned to California and Mac had drunk himself into a maudlin stupor. Dylan had helped him to his room. As he stumbled along, Mac had grinned at his son. "You're a good boy."

At the time she'd smiled at the use of the term boy when Dylan had been pushing thirty. Something told her Dylan had become a man much younger than most kids. "Your parents loved you, but taking care of Mac cost you a big chunk of your childhood."

Again, a pause. Daisy's laughter filtered in from the open family room.

"It is what it is." Dylan said. "There were some fun times."

When his mother was there, no doubt. When Daisy was between gigs and took time off from her lucrative career to spend time with Mac and Dylan. Jordan could picture her blowing in like Santa Clause, bearing a suitcase full of goodies.

When Jordan had lived here before, Daisy had arrived with expensive clothes for Mac, Dylan, and Jordan. Things that neither of the men would ever be caught dead in, but... Jordan had loved the beautiful silk scarf that had come in a bag from Rodeo Drive. Along with a pair of outrageous, dangly earrings that were more Daisy's style than Jordan's. Daisy had never met Jordan, but had included her in the event.

Dylan closed the dishwasher and glanced across the room. Jordan's parents were sitting stoically on the sofa while Daisy sat cross legged on the rug in front of the fire, playing with the twins as she chatted. "We'd better join the party."

They'd no more than sat down in the family room than her mother smiled at Dylan. "Jordan never mentioned that you were so domestic."

Dylan took the truck Trevor held out to him as Sam plopped down in front of the fireplace. "A lot of the time it was just me and Dad and the only thing he was good at in the kitchen was coffee. The man made a hell of a cup of coffee, but managed to burn water."

Jordan caught the fleeting frown that crossed Daisy's face, but she quickly hid it. Did she regret not being a fulltime mom to Dylan and wife to Mac? Jordan's father worked hard and earned a good living, but the house and meals were her mother's domain. The men in Dylan's family handled both.

Daisy snapped a red Lego together with a green one for Tristan. "Mac had many talents. Cooking wasn't one of them." Her laughter tinkled. "Now breaking high-spirited horses and women..."

Dylan shrugged. "I'm thinking he had a better track record with horses."

Nonplussed, Daisy turned to Jordan's mom. "Margaret is so formal. You look like a Maggie to me."

Mom's cheeks turned a pretty shade of pink. "Oh my, I haven't been called Maggie since my college days. Frank thinks Margaret is more suitable."

Daisy went to the stereo and searched the massive collection of CDs, plucked one out and slid it into the player. Suddenly Rod Stewart vibrated through the room, singing Maggie May. "I love classic rock. Had to teach Mac to appreciate anything other than George Jones, but it didn't take long."

Having grown up with classical cadence, Jordan was amazed when her mother's foot started tapping. "Oh to go back and relive my college days."

Jordan's dad flashed them all a frown and then turned his attention to Sam. No doubt disapproving of an animal in the house. He hadn't even allowed Jordan to have a yard dog.

"College wasn't my thing," Daisy said. "I skipped more classes than I showed up for. Then the summer I turned nineteen, my mom wanted me away from some of my 'friends' and sent me to Texas with my dad. He was a sound engineer on a movie they were filming in the Fort Worth stock yards. Mac was an extra in a rodeo scene. I took one look at those wide shoulders and that denim covered butt and that was the end of my college. When the filming ended, I stayed behind with Mac."

Daisy stood, closed her eyes and swayed to the beat as if she were dancing in her lover's arms.

"What did your parents think about that decision?" Jordan's father asked. "I'm sure they were not pleased."

"Oh, they mostly just wanted me to be happy. Thought Mac might settle me down. Mend my wild ways."

"Yeah, that worked out well." Sarcasm oozed from each word Dylan spoke.

Daisy danced her way over and kissed her son on his forehead. "Hey, you're here because of the passion between me and Mac. And you inherited his down to earth country sense while I balanced that with some free spirited ideals."

Free spirited enough to convince Jordan to hop on the back of his Harley and head to points unknown with no job and no plan of action. And Dylan had made it all work.

When they'd met, Dylan had been out of the army almost a year and was making his way across the country working odd jobs. He'd already built sets in California for a while before moving on to Colorado for the winter and landing a job leading snowmobile tours at a resort. Then when he and Jordan had moved to Florida he'd started out as a bouncer in a club, but soon found a job running a Jet Ski rental business where Jordan could be with him. He was a better rancher than his father and from all accounts had a natural instinct with horses. And women, Jordan thought remembering Daisy's comment about Mac.

Half asleep, Trevor crawled up onto his papa's lap and closed his eyes. Tristan had pulled the rocking horse out and was about to fall asleep from the rocking motion. Daisy scooped him up and danced him around the room.

There was an awkward lull in conversation, probably for lack of any neutral topic. Dylan cradled Trevor's head against his shoulder. The boy smacked on his thumb and drifted off into slumber.

Daisy slowed her sway to the music and Tristan also began to doze off in her arms. The music shifted to a deep country resonance. Daisy sniffed. "This was Mac's and my song. It's so hard to be in this house without him."

"I'll put Tristan to bed," Jordan offered, taking the boy from her. "You okay?"

Daisy swiped at the tears running down her cheeks. "I'm fine. I'll always have my memories."

Easing out of the chair, Dylan tried not to wake the sleeping boy. "You were his whole life, Mom."

"And he, mine."

Dylan patted her back then started toward the boys' room with Trevor. "Plowing the field with Papa is hard work."

Silently they each changed the boys' diapers and put them into sleepers. Jordan kissed each good night as Dylan did the same. He stood and rolled his head on his shoulders, loosening the stress. "Why don't you take my bed tonight. I can crash on the sofa."

She'd planned to share a room with Mom, but after Dad showed up, she'd given her parents the guest room. But she would never be able to sleep in Dylan's bed. "No need. I can bunk in with the kids."

They didn't need words to communicate what was on both their minds. Dylan's bed was big and they'd shared it many, many nights. But not anymore. Even if she could make him fall in love with her again, he'd never trust her. And she doubted there was anything she could do to get past that.

Chapter Fifteen

Knowing Jordan was in the next room kept Dylan wide awake all night. He gave up and rolled out of bed before the sun broke over the horizon. Lying there any longer was torture. His one consolation, best he could tell, she hadn't slept much more than he had. He'd heard every creak of the springs when she'd moved.

He padded into the kitchen, switched on the coffee pot, and then jumped in the shower. He couldn't sleep, but he wasn't quite awake either.

Coffee, crisp air, and chores helped, but after two sleepless nights, his eyeballs itched like a west Texas sand storm. Was he cursed to live the same life as his father, yearning for a woman two-thousand miles away? He knew Jordan cared for him on some level, but not the one that would make her want to pick up roots and stay here with him.

By the time Dylan made it back to the house, the women were bustling around like they had an agenda. Daisy poured a cup of coffee, topped it off with cream and handed it to him. "The women folk are going into Dallas for a spa day."

He raised his eyebrows at Jordan and took a sip of the milky coffee. She better not laugh. "You're going to drive an hour each way for a spa day?" Dylan asked.

Frank Harris frowned as Jordan placed her purse on the dining table. "You're going with them? Who'll watch the twins?"

Daisy leveled a cold blue glare on him.

Sam wisely flopped down on the rug in front of the sink, out of the line of fire. Daisy had no use for useless people. Dylan was with her on that.

He poured another cup of coffee, this one black, and said a prayer for stamina. Normally a day with the boys would be fun, but he had a pretty good idea that they'd had more sleep the night before than their mama and papa. "I've got 'em."

Jordan's eyes drooped and she didn't look up to a grueling Daisy type excursion. If she only had a clue what she was in for. The spa would be just the beginning. Daisy had dragged him around from shopping mall to shopping mall until he'd threatened to abandon her. Mostly she shopped and he and Dad had tagged along like pack mules to haul her loot.

"Have fun," he said to their departing figures. Trevor stood from his perch in front of morning cartoons. "Hosey."

"You want to ride Papa's horse?"

Trevor's blond curls fell in his face as his head bobbed up and down. "Now."

Plopping his cowboy hat on his head, Tristan grinned. Maybe he'd actually ride this time. Except that they were both still in their sleepers.

"You can't ride Cinder in those PJs. The dinosaurs might spook him."

"I'd like to have a few words with you first," Frank said.

This could be...painful. "Okay."

"I realize that you want Jordan and the twins to live here, but you must realize that a life in Connecticut would be best for them. I'm asking you, man to man, don't pull my daughter back into this."

Dylan tried to remain calm as he calculated the best angle of attack without getting into a heated argument. First off, it wasn't Frank's decision. And who the hell decided that Connecticut was a better place to grow up than Texas? But what struck him as almost funny was that the man believed that Dylan had the ability to draw Jordan into anything she didn't want to be drawn into. "Jordan is a grown woman. If it's all the same to you, she and I'll decide what's best."

Frank squeezed the bridge of his nose. "I knew it was asking too much for you to be reasonable."

"Reasonable? If I'm guessing right, you having Jordan's best interest at heart, cost me the first year and a half of my sons' lives. Pardon me if I don't really give a shit what you think."

The guy started to speak, but seemed to think better of it, snapped his mouth closed and disappeared into the study where his laptop had occupied the desk since his arrival.

"No need to get all huffy about it." Dylan said to his departing back, then turned his attention to the boys. Before he got their hopes up, he'd better call Rusty to see if he could enlist his help.

Once that was settled, dry diapers, jeans, shirts, jackets, and hats. Next time they came to visit, he'd buy them boots. "Ready to ride, guys?"

* * *

"And I thought Mac was intense! I swear, Maggie that man of yours would wear me down." As they pulled out of the drive, Daisy turned the car toward Dallas. "I hope you and Frank slept okay."

Mom smiled. "We slept fine. It's so peaceful out here. You don't hear sirens or city noises."

"Best times of my life were here with Mac." Daisy looked wistful. "We were fighting one minute and tearing off each other's clothes the next."

"Tore your clothes off?" Mom's eyes were as round as saucers. "I can't imagine Frank ever doing such a thing."

"Really?" Daisy put her hand over her mouth in mock disbelief.

Jordan watched Mom, but she didn't seem upset by Daisy's teasing. "I mean, things were different when we were first married, but even then Frank would take the time to fold his shirt and place it on the chair."

Jordan wanted to put her fingers in her ears. Like most children, she'd tried to avoid thinking about her parents as sexual beings. To hear her mom even allude to it seemed sort of strange and well, creepy.

"Now that's just wrong!" Daisy laughed. "I'd have torn his off just to see what he'd do. Those buttons would have gone bouncing. Mac always said I was hell on clothes just because I didn't take to his western shirts. But we won't talk about what he did to my clothes."

"Were you afraid of him?" Mom asked sounding like the naïve college coed to Daisy's more experienced role.

"Good lord no. Lots of passion, but he wouldn't hurt a flea. The arguments kept things interesting. Gave us an excuse to make up."

Mom turned and studied her new friend. "What did Mac think about you living in California?"

"Mac wanted me to be happy." Daisy's glossed lips turned up at the corners. "But as soon as I'd finish a job, I'd be on the next flight headed to Texas."

"Like a booty call?" Jordan asked.

Daisy didn't miss a beat. "Exactly."

* * *

Jordan sat on the wooden bench in the sauna alone with her mom, waiting for Daisy to finish her massage. The hot steam penetrated her pours. "I didn't realize how much I needed this."

"Did you know that Daisy and Mac made love the first day they met? When she told me, I almost choked." Mom tugged the lapels of her terry spa robe tighter.

Jordan leaned her head back against the wall, her face flushing into a smile. She could imagine quite easily, but she wasn't sure her mother could handle the truth closer to home.

Mom's head jerked around. "You didn't?" As reality penetrated, she shrugged. "McKeon males must possess some seductive aphrodisiac."

Jordan had lived with Dylan a year and they shared two kids, so Mom had to at least realize the relationship wasn't platonic. "Up until Dylan, I thought my friends were nuts for jumping into the sack on the first date. But then I met Dylan. The three days and nights he and I spent together were the most right thing I'd ever felt. I can't explain it. He taught me the beauty of making love."

Her mother rubbed her eyes. "So it was all physical?"

Wouldn't that have made things simple? "The evening after the snow mobile trek we were so busy getting to know one another, we never slept. All of us ended up at this little club for dinner. We danced. There was a light snow falling and it was so cold, but Dylan and I went for a walk. We talked about everything. One o'clock in the morning and we made snow angels and had a snowball fight. He was incredibly…sweet… and funny and…" Jordan took a breath and blinked back the beautiful memories. "By the time we got into that hot tub it was only a couple hours before sunup and he knew more about me than I'd ever shared with another living soul. And vice-versa."

Mom listened without comment.

"Remember the day I left home with Dylan? He was the first person to ever go toe to toe with Dad and win." Jordan shivered remembering the pure adrenaline she'd felt that day. "Mom, I know you said that Dad changed after you married, but did you ever love him like that? Like he was your whole life?"

Mom stared into the steam so long that Jordan wasn't sure she'd answer. "I loved him. But things change. He changed, but so did I. We let the magic get lost in the reality."

No way was Jordan willing for her life to turn out like her mother's. She couldn't love Dylan as desperately as she had and just watch it wither and die.

"Daisy says you and Dylan are soul mates, like she and Mac were." Mom stared directly into her eyes. "She says no matter how hard you two fight it, you'll never be over one another. That's why Mac wrote his will the way he did."

"Mac was a good man, but a bit misguided. I'm not sure he knew what he was doing."

"Maybe he knew his son loved you and he wanted him to be happy."

Jordan had left almost two years before Mac's death. If he'd thought that, seemed like he'd have given up that fantasy at some point.

"Dylan treated you like a princess, didn't he?"

"No." Jordan closed her eyes, uncomfortable having this intense of a conversation with her mother. "He treated me like a partner. Whatever we did, we decided together."

"And that's what you loved about him," her mother coaxed.

"Dylan's passion is what I loved about him. In Florida we never argued. Not once. Which may have something to do with why I don't know how to reason with him when he gets all worked up and starts yelling."

Mom dabbed at her forehead with the corner of her towel. "Maybe yell louder so he'll hear you?"

"I don't yell."

"Then kiss him." Daisy's voice startled Jordan. How long had she been standing there?

"Try it." Daisy dropped down across from Jordan on the other bench. "Take advantage of all that passion. I guarantee the whole scenario will take a different direction. Then talk after. He'll listen."

Jordan thought about all her training. Women need to talk and feel close before sex. Men feel more connected and close after. It hadn't worked that way for Dylan the other night. Or had it? Was that why he'd proposed?

"Dylan looks so much like his daddy. It blows my mind," Daisy said.

Jordan smiled. "Tristan is going to look like them too. I fear for whatever unsuspecting little girl falls under his spell."

Daisy stuck her legs out in front of her and wiggled her glossy fuchsia toenails. "Yes he does, but Trevor has Dylan's loving demeanor"

"Yeah." Jordan agreed. Trevor was born liking to cuddle. Much like his daddy. Even with all Dylan's yelling, there wasn't a mean bone in his body. "I think Tristan may have a bit of his grandmother Daisy in him. Always on the go and makes the most of whatever he's doing."

"Awww." Daisy grinned, but her thoughts seemed to be far away. She swiped at her eyes. "Hopefully by the next time I visit, Dylan will have moved into the master bedroom and I can sleep in one of the other rooms. I just toss around in that big ol' bed drowning in all the memories. I knew I'd miss Mac, but I wasn't prepared for this."

Jordan's throat tightened, but she tamped it down. Like Daisy, she'd spent night after sleepless night missing Dylan after she'd left the ranch. Though Dylan was still alive, Jordan's life was half a continent away from the man she loved. But that wasn't the main difference. Dylan's only interest in Jordan was to be close to his sons.

"It'll get easier with time." Jordan squeezed Daisy's shoulder. This woman who loved life had lost a big part of hers. Forever. "Maybe you should talk to Dylan. I know he's still trying to adjust to his father's death also."

She blotted her tears with the towel. "I can't."

* * *

They arrived back at the ranch after the first pampering day Jordan had had in two years, but she still wasn't relaxed. Daisy had made the arrangements and insisted on picking up the tab for all three women. Maggie Harris now sported bright pink nails and toes for the first time in Jordan's memory. What had happened to the poster woman for pearl pink?

"Attractive woman," Jordan's father said, ignoring his wife and looking out the window.

Jordan glanced out at Zoe and then turned away. She did not have to listen to this. The kids were napping and both grandmothers were here if they woke. "I'm going to check the mailbox."

"Thanks, sweetie," Daisy sing-songed from her perch in Mac's leather recliner.

Jordan grabbed Dylan's leather jacket off the peg by the door. Shoving her arms into it, she walked out of the house and headed down the gravel lane. It was half a mile to the main county road where the mailbox stood. She waved as she passed, but Dylan and Zoe were so absorbed in the horse that they neither one returned the gesture.

November in Texas. The leaves were just beginning to turn alongside the lane. At home the trees had been bare over a month. Maybe due to lack of sleep, but Jordan's senses were hypersensitive today. As she crossed the rickety bridge, she paused and looked down at the shallow water in the creek, crystal clear as it tumbled over the white rocks. The leaves along the bank were transitioning from green to rich russets and golds. The breeze ruffled her hair, but it wasn't cold, more brisk. She picked up a flat rock, remembering when Dylan had tried to teach her to skim rocks. Wrapping her pointer finger around the edge, she sailed it like a miniature Frisbee, but it hit the water with a thud and sunk. Like her love life.

This might be the last time she walked down this road, enjoyed the quiet. Would Zoe be living here soon? Dylan would move on. She couldn't imagine him being alone forever.

As she returned, she stopped beside Zoe and stared across the field where Dylan was riding the abused horse. A slow walk, but still, the animal was saddled and being ridden. "Impressive."

Zoe leaned against the fence. "The man or the horse?"

Okay, guess she'd set herself up for that. "Both, I guess. How did he do that?"

"He was patient, let the horse come to him." Zoe didn't turn from watching Dylan. "He has a natural gift. I can fix their physical wounds, but it takes someone with a special skill to heal the emotional."

Remembering the almost exact conversation from the night before regarding Mac, Jordan gulped. "And you're in love with him?"

Zoe turned, hands on hips. "Are you?"

The question struck her smack in the heart like a poison Cupid arrow. She deserved the other woman's blunt approach, but she wasn't sure how to answer.

Zoe shook her head. "Look, Jordan. Either love him like he deserves or cut him loose."

"I'm not holding him."

"Don't BS me." Zoe glanced at Dylan, probably to make sure he was still out of ear shot. "At the moment, Dylan is focused on you and his children, as he should be. Give him the same consideration."

"Did he take you to bed the first night you met?" Jordan blurted out before realizing just how crass that sounded. But it mattered. It mattered a lot. Mac and Daisy had slept together the first night as had Dylan and Jordan. Was she special or was that just common operating procedure for McKeon men? "I'm sorry. That was totally out of line."

Finally Zoe broke the stare and shook her head. "No. We took things a little slower."

Dylan turned the horse toward them and Jordan didn't want to be caught in a three way conversation. She wasn't calm enough to go back inside though, so made her way to the back porch swing. Zoe's truck left soon after, but Jordan stayed in the swing, absorbing the tranquility of her last Texas sunset. This time tomorrow she'd be touching down in Connecticut.

She stood from the swing as Dylan walked up from the barn. His gaze took a leisure trip the length of her torso. "Nice jacket."

The winter she'd lived here, she'd worn the jacket more than he had. *Keep the conversation light.* "Well, I always did look good in it."

He ran his hands up the leather arms and straightened the collar. "Gorgeous."

Flustered, Jordan took a step back. "I'd better check on the boys. They're probably up from their naps by now." But when she turned toward the door, she walked straight into her scowling father.

* * *

Jordan enjoyed having brought dinner home and not cooking. The problem didn't start until after the meal when her mom came out wearing a bright silk kimono. Her father could no longer hold his tongue. "What in God's name are you wearing?"

Mom twisted her hands then touched her new lounging outfit. "I can change."

"It's a kimono," Daisy piped in. "I think she looks lovely."

Dylan nodded. "That she does. I like the hair too."

Dad's eyes flashed, but his tone remained calm. "Is a kimono meant to be worn in a public setting?"

Holding out the skirt of her similar loungewear, Daisy was nonplussed. "We're family. It's not like she's headed out to church tonight. I offered to buy you a matching shirt," Daisy said to Frank, "But neither your wife nor daughter thought you'd wear it."

Dylan actually exchanged looks with her father. "Trust me, you wouldn't. You should check out some of the strange California getups in my closet."

Daisy shook her head at Dylan's plaid shirt. "Well, we all have our styles, but button down just didn't seem to suit Maggie. This new look is much softer."

Jordan slipped her arm around her mother. "You look ten years younger, Mom."

Tristan grinned as he touched the silky fabric. "Pretty."

Jordan tried to avoid looking into Dylan's eyes. It was just too difficult. Jordan's father on the other hand kept staring at her mother as if she'd grown a second head. Her new shorter haircut and highlights apparently were more change than he was capable of handling. Even the twins played quietly, picking up on the strange mood.

Other than her parents being there, the night could have been any other night. Sam stretched out in front of the fire. The Beach Boys were singing some surfer tune.

"Do you remember this song?" Daisy asked Dylan. "Your daddy hated it because I made the mistake of telling him that it was the first song I ever made love to."

Frank's head jerked around. Margaret remained quiet.

Dylan grinned. "I'm assuming Dad wasn't present for that little escapade."

"Oh he knew I'd been with other men before him, but he didn't like to be reminded. Always led to a fight." Daisy wiggled her eyebrows at Margaret. "Which always led to making up."

"You remember that story Grandma Anna always told?" Dylan asked. "You know, about when she was helping Grandpa fix the truck and he yelled at her, "Dammit, Darlin'!"

"Oh yes, and she told him that dammit and Darlin' did not belong in the same sentence." Daisy slapped her hands across her chest and her laughter tinkled through the room. "She turned and in the house she went. Then she decided not to let him get the last word and came back down and kissed him."

Dylan grinned at his mom. "Had the poor guy so confused, he didn't know what to do."

Daisy winked at Jordan. "From what I remember, they didn't accomplish a thing the rest of the day. Got out of bed as the sun was going down and scrambled eggs for dinner."

"Grandma was a hoot."

Jordan couldn't take her eyes off Dylan. He'd always had a contagious smile. And a deep timbre in his laughter.

He went to the kitchen to put the coffee pot on and returned with cups of milk for the kids.

The stereo changed to Springsteen and Daisy smiled at Dylan. "How many times have you danced to this song? Oh man, you moved just like the Boss."

Dylan sort of gyrated over and handed the kids their cups, then held out his hand to Daisy. She placed her hand in his and he pulled her to her feet. Jordan watched Dylan and his mom. They took dancing seriously, but when Jordan caught Dylan's eye, he glanced at her mother, reading Jordan's mind. Just like old times.

"Tristan. Trevor. Get up and help your old man out. There are three women who need dancing with."

As the kids bounced to their feet, Dylan held his hand out to Jordan's mom. "Do me the honor?"

Mom's cheeks flushed, but she took Dylan's hand and joined him in the center of the room.

Jordan and Daisy each picked up a baby. Jordan had never seen her mother like this, rocking out to Springsteen. Who knew? Her mother was a pro at a waltz or slow dance. But this?

Feeling sorry for her father, Jordan turned the twins over to Daisy and reached for his hand. "Dance with me, Daddy."

Without hesitation, he stood and moved into formal dance position. He danced her away from the others before speaking. "Jordan, I love you. But what are you doing here?" He indicated the log outer walls on the house. "This isn't the life I raised you for. This isn't what I want for you. I think you should want better for your sons."

Blinking back tears, she leaned her head against his shoulder. I, I, I. This was still all about him and what he wanted. Yes, she knew he loved her. But his brand of love involved giving her what *he* thought she should have and preparing her for the life *he* thought would be best. Not once had he ever asked her what she wanted.

"Don't you think I want the best schools for the boys? I will provide everything they need." Jordan froze. In her determination not to become as dependent as her mother, had she instead become her father? Was she making all the decisions based on what *she* wanted?

* * *

Dylan excused himself and went to the kitchen to serve coffee. Jordan was still dancing with her father, deep in conversation, but her mom followed Dylan. "Can I help?"

"Sure, you can fix your and Frank's coffee."

Taking two mugs, Margaret focused on them. "Being here with you and your mother, I've realized that I did Jordan an injustice. I shouldn't have allowed her to grow up believing that giving in to her emotions and fighting for her own dreams was bad."

Dylan closed his eyes. "I'm not sure you can teach someone not to feel. They either do or they don't."

She turned and faced him. "Dylan, you need to hear this. I was Jordan's coach when the twins were born. During the night she was struggling to feed one of them and she thought I was asleep. She was crying and asking herself what she'd done?"

"She should've told me." He tried to swallow.

"Yes, she should have. But Frank convinced her you weren't the type father a child needed. You had no job. No goals. He offered his support to help her finish her Masters. Convinced her that she could give the boys a better life without you."

He grasped the edge of the countertop and gritted his teeth. "None of that would have mattered if she had loved me like I loved her. I'd have followed her anywhere, if she'd asked. But she didn't. She didn't even tell me she was leaving. No matter what Frank did or said, Jordan made the choice."

Margaret took a deep breath and closed her eyes, then opened them and stared straight into his. "When Jordan was about twelve, she walked in on Frank and me arguing. I demanded things my way and he insisted on his. When I continued to argue, he reminded me that the door swung both ways, but asked how I thought I could support myself without him. After all, he earned his degree and made good money, but after we got married I dropped out of college and ran the house. I stomped to the closet and yanked down my suitcase, but as I turned, I caught sight of Jordan standing in the doorway. The horror on my daughter's face made my decision. That was the last time I ever really confronted Frank. He gave us everything we needed, whether it was exactly what we wanted or not."

Dylan remembered hearing his own parents argue, but he'd been so used to it that it was just a way of life. They argued. They made up. Life went on. "But Jordan has a degree. And we never argued about money."

"She was only twenty-two. So young and impressionable. And pregnant."

"Right and she's now twenty-five and the mother of two." He shrugged. "Look, I asked her to marry me. She turned me down. I'm done."

Chapter Sixteen

As hard as he tried, Dylan couldn't get Margaret Harris' words out of his mind. Even after everyone had turned in, he stared at the fire, listening to the rhythmic ticking of Grandmother's clock and Springsteen's sexy lyrics. He stoked the logs, watching the sparks in the dark. Had Jordan loved him? Regretted not telling him?

He wasn't sure what to believe.

Sensing movement, he found Jordan standing beside him.

"You okay?" she asked.

He stared at her. Navy silk pajamas with white flowers hung loose on her slender figure, but he glimpsed cleavage in the V-neckline. Margaret's words kept playing over in his mind like a scratched record. "One more time. Why did you leave me?"

The flames made her golden brown eyes flash with color. "Why didn't you come after me?"

"So it was a game?"

"Dylan, you told me to leave."

"We had a fight and you left to see if I'd chase you?" This was nuts. "It was an argument. That's what people do. They argue. They work things out."

"Rational adults don't argue. They discuss."

He punched the button on the stereo and turned off Springsteen who was obviously on fire. "So you left a damn note and took off without talking to me. That's your idea of rational adult behavior?"

"If I had stayed, we'd have ended up back where we started. We were making each other miserable."

"It was pretty damn good when we started."

She shook her head. "Florida was a fantasy. You and I don't do reality."

He could feel his teeth grinding. "Reality check. I won't spend my life like my father, pining over a woman who doesn't love me enough to even live in the same state."

"Don't blame me for your parents' odd lifestyle."

"Hell, at least my parents lived." He cocked an eyebrow. "You'd better get some sleep. Early flight tomorrow."

* * *

One o'clock in the morning and she hadn't shut her eyes. Jordan moved Trevor over so she had room to stretch out, but it wasn't crowding into the twin bed with her son that kept her awake. The bed springs in the next room creaked as Dylan turned over, yet again. Apparently he couldn't sleep either.

The pipes sang as the shower turned on and the shower curtain rings scraped across the metal rod.

She rubbed her eyes. This was the last night they would be in the same house together, possibly forever. There was no future for them as a couple, yet there was a past. And a present.

She stood in the center of the room, staring at the bathroom door. Dylan was naked, in the shower.

Bending down, she pulled the cover over her sleeping son. Trevor rolled over and stuck his thumb in his mouth. She walked across the room toward the bathroom.

Opening the door, she was careful not to make a sound.

What was she doing?

She'd be gone tomorrow!

She eased the door closed behind her and leaned against it as Dylan held the shower curtain back. His eyes stared through the steam into hers and she didn't look away.

When he didn't speak, didn't tell her to leave, she slowly stepped out of her pajama bottoms.

This was insanity.

Still, they held each other's gazes.

Just for tonight.

And then she could let him go.

It only took a few seconds to unbutton her pajama top and drop it to the floor with its mate.

Dylan held the curtain back and she stepped beneath the hot, pelting spray. Closing her eyes, she ran her hands up his familiar chest, to his shoulders and neck. His lips warm as they took possession of hers, soft, penetrating, demanding more. She should keep her eyes closed, but the desire to see Dylan was stronger. He leaned his head back and let the spray comb his thick hair back, then his lips returned to hers. "I need to get protection."

She nibbled his lip and laced her fingers through the wet hair at his nape. "I took care of that."

He groaned, then cupped her bottom and coaxed her legs around his waist. As the hot shower spray pelted their bodies, her bare back landed gently against the cold tile. All she could think was how desperately she wanted him. Taking one of her hands in each of his, he held them above her head as he entered her. There was such rightness about being with Dylan. She closed her eyes and held on, reveling in each sensation, each movement. The strength in his thighs as he effortlessly supported her weight. The width of his shoulders, and those abs. Her body perfectly tuned to his every thrust. She squeezed her legs tightly around him and held on for the ride. Wrapping her arms around his neck, she grasped his shoulders and nipped his dark nipple. She panted faster and faster as he pumped. Reveling in the feel and scent of Dylan. He tossed his head back as he came, bringing her along with him.

Her emotions soared and her body trembled. His thighs quivered beneath her weight and she slid to her feet, spiraling downward into a deep dark oblivion.

* * *

Dylan made coffee before five and headed out to take care of the chores. He had hardly closed his eyes anyway. After Jordan left, he was going to sleep for a week straight.

Mid-November and the early morning fog hung heavy over the property, adding to the eerie mood. He couldn't even see the barn until he was right on it. Temperature had dropped twenty degrees overnight.

What the hell was he supposed to make of that whole shower scene? No explanation. Jordan had just made love like there was no tomorrow then disappeared as silently as she'd appeared. Had he imagined it? Given the lack of sleep lately, he wouldn't be surprised.

Maybe if he got done early, he'd have time to feed the boys breakfast before Jordan hustled them off to the airport. No telling when he'd get to see them again.

Opening the barn door, his eyes strayed to the hay loft where he and Jordan had made love one rainy afternoon. His dad had passed out and the house had been closing in on her. She'd arrived with a couple of beers rolled up in a blanket. They'd made love before falling asleep to the sound of rain peppering the metal roof.

Cinder nuzzled his hand and the feel of Jordan riding behind him on the stallion moved into focus. She'd never gotten past her fear of horses, but had ridden with him a few times.

God, was there anything that didn't bring back some memory of her? When he rode the Harley, he could swear he felt her behind him. Snow reminded him of the ski resort in Colorado where they'd met. Humidity reminded him of Florida and the summer they'd lived there. His bed. The house. Hell she now owned half of the ranch.

He patted Sam's head. Even the dog had been a gift for Jordan after she'd mentioned that she was never allowed to have a pet.

Just get to the chores, McKeon.

* * *

It wasn't even seven AM when Dylan returned. The house looked ghostly through the fog, lit up like a party. He had to step around the stack of luggage on the porch waiting to be loaded into the airport van that had just arrived. Frank Harris had insisted that the van was a better option than Dylan's king cab pickup. The twins had too much stuff he'd said. But seven AM? The flight didn't leave for four more hours.

Yet when Dylan walked in, everyone already had on their coats. Jordan and her

Mother had their purses in hand. The boys sat on the sofa, well-scrubbed, hair slicked down, and dressed in matching tan slacks and burgundy golf shirts. The only difference was that Trevor's windbreaker was navy and Tristan's was forest green.

Had Jordan planned to sneak off without giving him a chance to tell the kids goodbye? His jaw tightened. She could have called his cell and let him know that her father was rushing things along. Ignoring her, he knelt down and held his arms out to the kids. "Hey guys. Come give Papa a hug."

Trevor flung himself into Dylan's arms and wrapped his tiny arms around his neck so tight it was hard to breathe. Dylan cradled him with one arm and wrapped the other around Tristan, standing patiently to the side. God, was it always going to hurt this bad to tell them goodbye?

Frank stepped inside. "Shuttle's waiting. Ready?"

He might be, but Dylan wasn't. He hoisted both twins up and followed Jordan out to the white airport van. Tristan tuned up to cry as Dylan sat them down on the driveway. He remembered how he'd felt the many times his mom had left. *Just smile*. This wasn't their fault and there was no need to upset them more.

He knelt beside them and kissed the tip of his finger, then placed it to Tristan's lips. "Love you."

Tristan returned the gesture, then fell into his arms. Dylan squeezed him tight, then buckled him into his car seat. "Papa will come see you soon. Promise."

He hugged Trevor who appeared more confused than upset as he buckled him into his seat. Dylan had been older when his Mom had moved him away from the ranch to live in California, but he could relate to the confusion. It was like having two homes, but not belonging at either. Which was one reason that after a month he'd chosen to move back to the ranch and live with his father permanently.

He forced a smile. "Love you, son. You guys be good on the plane for Mama."

Margaret hugged Daisy and climbed into the third seat in the van as Daisy smothered each baby with hugs and kisses. Jordan stood to the side and waited, looking very businesslike. Hard to fathom this woman wearing black slacks and a black and gray sweater, her hair clipped back severely from her face, was the same sex goddess who'd backed him against the shower wall six hours earlier.

She extended her hand to him. "I appreciate you allowing me to be here with the boys. Just let me know when you'd like to come visit them."

That was it? Allowing her to be here with the boys? They hadn't resolved a thing. Like he had to ask her permission to see his own kids. She wouldn't meet his eyes. This was bullshit. He stuffed his hands into his pockets. "See you in court."

Dylan turned and went back inside. Watching the van leave carrying Jordan and the twins ripped his heart out and twisted his insides into a knot. If possible, this was worse than the first time Jordan had left him on that icy morning in Colorado after Spring Break. Then, they'd known each other all of three days and yet it had felt like that silver plane was sucking the life out of him as it had backed away from the jet bridge and disappeared into a cloud of snow, carrying Jordan back to Connecticut.

His mother followed close on his heels, waving toward the open door. "You're just going to let her leave?"

"Why the hell not? She didn't even tell me they were leaving early so I could say goodbye to the boys."

Daisy cocked her eyebrow at him. The one he always wanted to hold down when he was a kid because it meant she was about to say something he didn't want to hear. "Hmm, maybe that explains why your cell phone is vibrating on the nightstand."

Patting his pocket, he groaned. Given his sleep deprived state, figured that he'd left without it this morning.

"Dylan, don't be a fool. You're in love with Jordan."

"Doesn't matter." He massaged his pounding temples. "My heart says I should stay in the fight, but my mind argues that it's time to cut my losses and let it go."

"Listen to your heart."

"Oh, would that be the same heart that a bull just trampled?" He stared at the rocking horse beside the fireplace. "She doesn't love me, at least not enough to stay with me and raise the boys. I'm forced to play the long distance game with my kids, but I won't play it with Jordan. Either she marries me and stays here or we aren't together."

"A signature on a piece of paper can't guarantee that." She dropped down on the sofa and clasped her hands. "If you love something or someone, you make it work."

Dylan shook his head. Hard to make it work when Jordan wasn't willing. "Mom, don't take this wrong, but I don't want the kind of relationship like you and Dad had."

She stared at him. "Because you blame my actions for Mac's death?"

This was not a good time to delve into a lifetime of crazy. "For years I blamed you for his alcoholism. But you can't change what another person does, only your reaction to it." He visualized Jordan sitting at the kitchen table saying pretty much those exact words one afternoon when Mac had stumbled off to bed, drunk. "Dad's drinking started as a crutch for the pain from his rodeo injuries. Then he drank as a way to deal with missing you. But even when I tossed all the alcohol, he continued to find more. He was hell bent and determined to drink himself into an early grave no matter what you or I did."

"It wasn't fair of me to leave you to deal with that." Daisy stood and wrapped him in her arms, tears streaming down her cheeks. "I love you and I loved your father. Part of me died with him."

"I know." Dylan ran his hands down her back. "He loved you, Mom. When you were here, the house was happy, he was alive. You were his life."

"But when I wasn't...You think I should have cut him loose?"

He backed away and shrugged. "I thought he should have cut you loose. But then I realized that you were what kept him going."

Daisy took his face between her hands. "I never married Mac, but in thirty-three years together, I never had any desire to sleep with another man."

He gulped. He knew his father hadn't wanted other women, even when they'd blatantly pursued him. But he'd always figured Daisy's California life included other lovers. "That worked for you guys, but I'm not willing to live like that and Jordan isn't willing to commit. To fight for us."

"Looking back, maybe I shouldn't have taken the job in California. But you and your father were always number one with me."

Daisy was an in the moment person. Wherever she was and whatever she was doing was the number one priority at that moment. It wasn't exactly a fault, just her mode of operation. "I do love you, Mom."

She kissed his cheek. "I love you too. All I want is your happiness."

He winked. "I'm a grown man. I'll figure it out."

* * *

Jordan lifted each twin into a molded airport chair and took a seat between them. Her arms ached from juggling kids, diaper bags, car seats, and all the paraphernalia required when traveling with toddlers. She couldn't shake the feeling of doom that had come over her the minute that van had pulled away from the ranch. *I'll see you in court.* It wasn't the words, but how Dylan had said them. He hadn't raised his voice. But she sensed a deeper anger than she'd ever heard in his yelling.

Tristan slid out of the seat and grabbed the stuffed rabbit Trevor cherished. Before Jordan could recover the rabbit, Trevor wailed, "Mine!"

Her dad flashed a stern look. "They need to settle down. They're in public."

Jordan recovered the rabbit and handed it to Trevor. "I'm doing the best I can."

Dad kept his voice low so he didn't seem angry, just out of sorts. "I know. Didn't take them long to pick up their father's ways. They're already showing the effects of being exposed to his crazy family."

"Get off Dylan's case. Whether we're together or not, he's an excellent father." Jordan picked up Tristan and her mother scooped Trevor and the bunny up.

Mom shrugged. "Well crazy or not, there was love in that home. Daisy is devastated by Mac's death."

Dad checked the time on the tickets, slid them neatly into his breast pocket, then turned to Mom. "You can't honestly think that hot headed cowboy and his family know anything about love. His father died of acute alcoholism and his mother is some flower child. Daisy Zimmerman didn't even love Mac McKeon enough to commit to a marriage."

"There are all kinds of loving relationships," Mom replied. "I'd give anything to have the depth of emotion in Daisy and Mac's relationship and that I see in Jordan and Dylan." Mom met Dad's glare, eyeball to eyeball.

Dad took the seat beside his wife. "What exactly are you saying? You can't possibly prefer what they had over us."

Mom ran her fingers through Trevor's blond curls. "I'm not sure what I want. I'm going to start with a job."

For once, Dad didn't have a response.

"A real job, with a paycheck," Mom continued.

"So you can move out? I can't imagine anything you could want that I haven't given you. I've worked my tail off for us to have a nice home, clothes, and new cars. A perfect life."

"Well, maybe a perfect life isn't so perfect. I don't want a silver Mercedes. I want a little yellow convertible. And remember how we went cross country skiing in college?"

He looked stunned. "Okay...we...I...I never realized how you...we can do that."

Jordan had fallen into an alternate universe. Nobody was who she thought they were. The only person who made sense was Daisy. She missed Mac, simple. But Mom was talking like a college kid, about goals and dreams. Her parents were arguing. Jordan wasn't even sure her mother wouldn't file for divorce.

She held tight to Tristan, but she couldn't focus. A million thoughts tumbled chaotically through her brain. Daisy. Dylan. He loved his mother, but she'd hurt him. Every time Jordan and Dylan argued and he challenged her to leave, was it just that insecure little boy inside him testing to see if she too was going to desert him?

But this time when she left, something had been different. The look on Dylan's face. Cold acceptance. Had she managed to push him away with such finality that he had no feelings left?

Her hand shook as she bent to retrieve Tristan's fire truck. She couldn't stop the trembling as it spread from her hands until her entire body shook. Tears pooled behind her eyes.

Tristan twisted and climbed up in her face. He kissed the tip of one tiny finger and pressed it to her lips. "Love you."

Jordan gulped. Just like he'd seen his father do. Just like Dylan had done to her when she'd been upset about burning some silly stir fry and smoking up their tiny apartment in Florida. Her Dylan. The same Dylan who had just said goodbye to her with a total lack of emotion.

Dylan happy, absolutely. Dylan angry, oh yeah. Dylan in the grips of passion... But Dylan emotionless! What had he said that time when they were arguing? That as long as he was yelling, they were communicating. That she should worry when he got quiet. She hadn't gotten it, but her mother had. Arguing doesn't mean a relationship is going bad, it means one cares enough to fight for it. Had Jordan even tried?

Oh my god. The one thing she always tried to change about Dylan, his emotions, was the exact thing that made her fall in love with him.

She stared out the picture windows at the planes taking off. What was she doing? This was wrong. She had to fight for the man she loved.

Stuffing the toys and cups into the boys' diaper bag, she looked into her mother's eyes. "I've got to go back."

"Yes!" Mom started zipping Trevor into his jacket. "Remember what Daisy said."

"Just kiss him." Frantically, Jordan tried to load everything into her arms. "I need a car. I need the boys' luggage. Never mind, just ship it to me."

"Here, I've got this." Mom swung the diaper bag over her arm, then turned to Dad. "Are you going to call the shuttle back for her?"

Dad grabbed one of the car seats and pulled out his cell phone. "I'm on it."

* * *

Dylan walked up from the barn, planning to crawl into bed and tune it all out. No sleep, dealing with Jordan's parents, and his mom, plus saying goodbye to the kids. Not to mention struggling with his feelings for Jordan. Days like today he regretted giving up dri--.

Jordan stood in the center of the kitchen.

He blinked, swallowed. He should start locking the door.

Without a word, she sauntered toward him. Standing on her bare tiptoes, she moved to kiss him.

He held both hands out to the side, refusing to touch her. "What kind of game are you playing?"

"I'm not."

"The hell you aren't!" He tossed his hat on the table and noticed remnants of the kids' lunch on their little table. "Where are the boys?"

"Napping." She took a breath. "Dylan, I love you. I've always loved you."

"Don't. You want to live in Connecticut and turn my kids into little preps. Go back to the airport."

She didn't flinch. Didn't back away. She looked around. "I own half this ranch. The boys and I are staying. If you don't want to be here with us, then you leave."

"What?" She chose now to play that trump card? "You hate this ranch!"

"It's growing on me." She cocked her head to the side. "I love you. Leaving you left a crater the size of Texas inside me. You remember what you said about us never being done with one another? Well, I pray that's true because I never want to live without you, Dylan McKeon. I want our names on a marriage license, rings on our fingers, the whole gambit."

Don't trust her. "What about your internship?"

She arched a dark eyebrow. "With all these hot-headed Texans, some of them are bound to need a therapist."

"This is nuts! You said..."

Suddenly she was in his arms and her mouth was on his. Her lips hot, moist and searching. Her breasts flattened against his chest. Her hands on his ass, pressing him tight against her. He should put an end to this... As soon as things got rough, she'd leave again.

But...her tongue was in his mouth.

Placing his hands beneath her curvy little ass, he struggled to haul her to the bedroom. She wasn't much help as she locked her legs around his waist and continued her assault on his mouth.

Tumbling backwards onto the bed, he brought her along for the ride. Before he could get her shirt off, she pushed him back against the pillows and straddled him. "I know the only reason you want to marry me is because of the twins, but you're in my soul, Dylan, so…"

Focus, McKeon. "What?"

"I didn't think I could stand that. Being married to you and knowing you didn't love me would be worse than my mom's predicament because I don't think she loved Dad. But I'm not going to give up until you love me as much as I love you."

His heart stopped, then pounded against his chest. She started to kiss him again, but he slid his hand from beneath her shirt and held her away long enough to open the nightstand drawer and pull out the jeweler's box. "Just read the name on the box."

She took the black velvet jeweler's box and opened it, shaking her head. "Keys Jewelers." The second the reality penetrated, her expression melted. "You bought this ring when we were living in Florida? In the Keys?"

He swallowed a lump in his throat. "I knew you were the one that first night in Colorado. But I couldn't ask you to be my wife until I got my life together. Had a real income. Then Dad called and Texas happened and things went south." He closed his eyes, then opened them and stared into hers. "And then you left."

Her hand shook and tears streamed down her face. "I think the intensity of that first night we made love scared us both."

"My life has never been the same." He slipped the solitaire onto her finger, then rested a hand against her cheek and wiped the tear with his thumb. "God I love you, Jordan."

The gold flecks in her eyes flashed as did her dimple as she studied the ring. "I just have to learn to stand up to you when you get all crazy and emotional."

He narrowed one eye. "And I have to learn not to strangle you when you get all rational and self-righteous."

"I'm not self-ri..."

He cut her off with a kiss. "Yeah, you are, but I love you that way."

He yanked his shirt over his head and reached for her, but she'd already stripped off her blouse and jeans, leaving only her panties and a silky camisole. He shucked his shirt and boots, rolled her over and took control of the lovemaking. He needed her and he needed her now.

"Papa." Tristan's voice jarred him back to reality.

Jordan quickly scrambled to an upright position and adjusted her camisole.

So much for hot and heavy. Dylan scooped the boy up and deposited him on the king sized bed. "Hey, kiddo."

Jordan lifted Trevor up to join the family.

Dylan grinned at her. "So this is the way it's going to be?"

She laughed. "Apparently so."

Dylan tickled Trevor. "We're going to have to work on your timing, son."

Partners By Design (Coming June 2013)

What? What did he want from her? Savannah strained her neck to study his face, decipher his thoughts. Navy blue eyes burned into hers, but he waited. Why didn't he touch her?

I shouldn't want him to touch me.

His hands were inches from where her shirt gaped open. If she turned just slightly.

Tilting her head against his shoulder, she nuzzled in and rubbed her nose against his neck, inhaling a whiff of rain, sweat, and musky aftershave.

We can't do this.

Don't turn me away.

His mouth covered hers, lips parted, inviting her inside the warmth. His fingers undid the two buttons she'd managed to fasten on the shirt then squeezed her breast. He slid his other hand beneath her hair, his fingers pressing hot as he repositioned her for a deeper kiss.

She tugged on his damp hair, pulling him closer and feasting on his mouth, starved for the once-familiar taste of Logan. His ten o'clock shadow scratched her chin and ignited her peaked senses.

Thunder rumbled and clashed across the sky and sheets of rain washed over the truck. Deep in the floorboard her phone vibrated, but she tuned it out.

Logan tasted so right. The years melted away. She was sixteen again, and carefree, and alive. She'd missed this. Missed him.

Logan Reid was the long awaited sequel to her own personal teenage love story. The one she'd replayed in her mind so many times she'd never forgotten a single line of dialogue or erotic sensation. But she'd rewritten the ending hundreds of times.

"Come home with me."

Her eyes popped open and she blinked at Logan. Familiar yes, but not the young boy of her fantasies.

They weren't teenagers and she was not going to let him destroy her again. In desperation, she pushed away and tugged her shirt together. "What made me ever think we could be friends?"

Circling her waist with his hands, he pulled her back against his bare chest, and rested his chin on top of her head. "You were the best friend I ever had, Savannah." His lips nibbled her ear and his breath tickled her neck. "You were everything good that ever happened to me."

His words cut deep into her memories. She'd felt the same. But that was before he'd left her cold and alone with not a single word of explanation beyond, 'It's over.'

ABOUT THE AUTHOR

Pamela Stone spent twenty plus years in the technology field before becoming a romance writer. She is a native Texan whose mom encouraged the importance of wardrobe, dance, and piano lessons and whose father added go-kart racing, slot cars, water skiing, and a pony to the mix. Toss in a wild imagination, lazy walks on her grandparent's farm and another grandmother with a shed full of romance novels to while away hot afternoon.

Writing is pure escapism for Pamela. Childhood imaginary friends grew into teenage fantasies. Later as a mother of two young boys, she began writing to keep in touch with the adult world. She continued writing as a method to wind down in the evenings from long days spent in Corporate America. Anybody notice a pattern here? Not enough adult socialization – write. People overload – write. Either way, she claims that writing keeps her sane. Cheaper than a therapist and tons more fun.

She still resides in Texas with her childhood sweetheart and husband. She loves writing romance and sold her first novel, Last Resort: Marriage, on Friday the 13th, June 2008. How's that for luck!

Pamela loves to hear from her readers and can be reached through her website at: www.pamelastone.net

Made in the USA
Charleston, SC
28 June 2013